MW01054114

Tobe and the River Is

A Strange and Most Peculiar Tale

Story and artwork by Micah Sanger
with drawings from Tobe's sketchbook

I found this book floating in the River Is.

It is Its gift to *you*.

Tobe and the River Is
by Micah Sanger
www.4riveris.com and www.perception4u.com

ISBN: 978-0-9970525-0-3 (paperback)
          Library of Congress Control Number: 2016932768

Published 2016
Second Edition 2018
© 2016 by Micah Sanger

All rights reserved. No part of this publication may be reproduced, distributed, or transmitted in any form or by any means, including photocopying, recording, or other electronic or mechanical methods, without the prior written permission of the author, except in the case of brief quotations embodied in critical reviews and certain other noncommercial uses permitted by copyright law. Permission requests should be mailed to the author via email: micahperception@gmail.com

Other formats: 978-0-9970525-1-0 (hardback)
                     978-0-9970525-2-7 (EPUB)
                     978-0-9970525-3-4 (Mobi)
                     978-0-9970525-4-1 (PDF)
                     978-0-9970525-5-8 (audio)

Cover art, interior illustrations, and drop caps: Micah Sanger
Interior design: www.MediaNeighbours.com

Printed in the United States of America

25 24 23 22 21 20 19 18   2 3 4 5

To you and to the living River Is—
the source of all life and joy.

Contents

Preface

WHAT DO YOU THINK is our greatest need and challenge in this life? What affects us and those with whom we interact most directly? Is it not our movement into our spiritual nature? Is it not also the revelation of love that this movement brings?

Through the character of Tobe in this book, we learn of this transition into spirit and Self. Through him, we also see how to bring into harmonious balance this physical life with higher dimensions of experience. We see, too, the transformation of his world as he looks upon it with new eyes alight with the touch of spirit. Come, join Tobe on his revealing, startling journey, which in reality is your own.

"Come, ride the River Is.
It will change your life and fill it with wonder!"
Auriel

CHAPTER ONE

Where It All Begins

*We stand in mere wonderment, and the best part of things is
closed to us. We all walk in mysteries. We are surrounded by
an atmosphere in which we know not what is stirring, or how it
is connected with our own spirit.*

Johann Wolfgang von Goethe

 VEN WHEN YOUNG, TOBE (Tō·bē) did not fear the Great
Nothing. He loved its darkness. As he looked about at
his world bathed in light, everything stood out more
clearly before the vast darkness of the Great Nothing.
Everything appeared more alive and even more amazing. He was not like many who quaked before its
mystery, letting their fears write upon it. Nor did he
entertain himself with frightening stories about what
crouched and crawled within its dark folds.

When young, Tobe's eyes, as the eyes of all new living things in the
world, were full of sparkle. They glowed with the light of a world beyond,
the world from where he came. His little-boy heart, too, was huge. In its
vast space, it gently held everything he looked upon.

But, over the years, that space had withered and become small from
all the concerns and doubts of living in the world. His heart, too, became
cluttered with a thousand useless things—the kinds of things we all gather
as the years go by—the clutter we don't even notice growing, until it is impossible to move freely about within ourselves.

So without knowing when or how it happened, Tobe had gone from believing anything was possible to believing chiefly in what he could touch with his hands and see with his own eyes. For the most part, he had become a "practical" young man. From this place, he reached out and gathered what simple pleasures he could from his world. And what gave him the most pleasure was to be out on his boat, fishing and doodling in his sketchbook.

"You're in early today, Tobe," said Goran, quickly glancing up from wrapping three pounds of minnows in paper for a customer. The lady dropped a few coins into Goran's hand and, smiling, departed with her package. It was a little after midday, and the market was a flurry of activity.

Goran turned to Tobe, whose handcart was filled with baskets overflowing with golden minnows, and said, "Nice-looking catch."

Tobe pulled his handcart closer to the scales and the ice tables—ice brought down each morning from the higher peaks.

Tobe had to speak loudly so his friend could hear. "It was a good morning with a light drizzle and only a wisp of a breeze coming from the north. You could feel the pressure in the air falling. The minnows went right into the nets, as if they were the honored guests going to a ball. By high morning, the threat of a storm had blown over, but by then all was done."

"They will bring a good price," said Goran, struggling to lift a basket from the cart onto the scales.

Tobe smiled with a flush of satisfaction, looking at the prize-filled cart. Then a delightful thought crossed Tobe's mind. "Goran, I've got to get running. Kallee is in the upper meadow." Unable to contain his enthusiasm, he stripped off his tattered outer fishing clothes and tossed them to the ground. "If I hurry, I can catch her. We'll settle up later, Goran. I trust you more than a brother."

Goran dropped another basket on the scales with a loud grunt. He studied Tobe, smiling. He could remember when he was once in love. "Have a good run, Tobe. And pace yourself; you have a long way to go." He knew Tobe loved to run—almost as much as he loved to be out on the water.

Tobe took in a long-drawn breath and sprang into a trot and then into a sprint. He dashed through the market—an obstacle course of tents, people, and carts—jumping over crates and barrels as he went. Yes, how he loved to run. He felt powerful; nothing could stop him. There was no separating him from his simple joy; they were one.

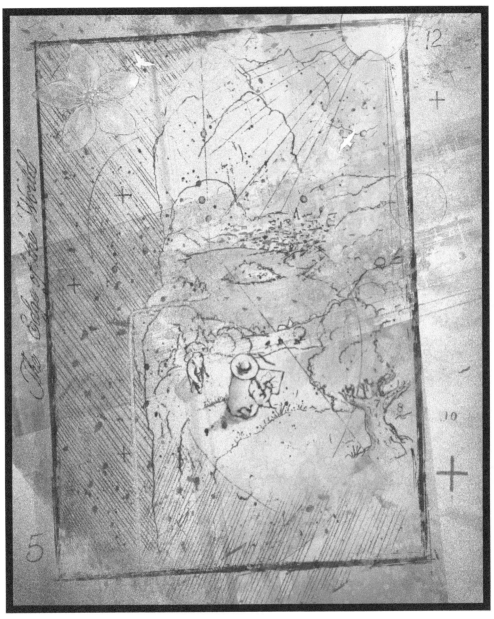

Self Portrait and the Edge of the World.
Written in Tobe's sketchbook underneath this drawing are these
words: "Standing before the vast Great Nothing, the beauty of this
world shines; now I begin to fathom its mystery."

Down the alleyways of Soñadora he ran. The sound of his feet echoed off the stones. He raced through canyons of whitewashed walls meandering up all willy-nilly, two to three stories high, topped with red-tiled roofs and chimneys with faint wisps of smoke. Nowhere was there a straight line on window, door, or wall. He made his way back down to the pier, his fast and nimble feet thumping on wood planks, until, halfway down, he leaped to the sand on the lake's edge.

His breathing grew deeper. A fire grew in his veins. The exhilaration of running filled him. It seemed as if he were defying the laws of space, bending space to his will with his long, quick strides.

Gravity, too, seemed to let go its firm hold for a moment, as he leaped like a gazelle over shrubs and rocks with pure ease, sometimes as high as his own height. Flight, he was sure, was just a small miracle away, a sprinkle of wonder away. Yet, just as it seemed that gravity's firm hold might be undone and he would finally soar free, his feet would come thudding back to the ground as he ran on.

As he jogged, he glanced to the west at the blue, sparkling lake. A little farther on, the hills and rocks came to an abrupt end before the vast, dark wall of the Great Nothing began. The height and width of this darkness extended far beyond what Tobe could see.

The edge of the world!

To see the landscape of Soñadora all bathed in sunlight before the blackness of the Great Nothing took Tobe's breath away.

What is this mysterious world we live in for a while? He expected no answer and he got none. Being filled with wonder was enough for him. His mind cleared once again, and he could hear his quick, running steps cutting through the sand.

The smell of aquatic plants was sharp. Little waves lapped on the shore. The voices of the fishermen in their boats echoed off the water, where they were busy with their catch of golden minnows, the only fish to be found in the lake's deep, cool waters. Those who saw him, waved to Tobe as he passed.

On any day, it was common to see thirty or more dories, painted in brilliant yellow, red, green, or blue, floating on the lake's surface. Tobe loved it when the wind picked up and the dories bobbed and rolled, creating a rhythmic dance with the swaying trees on the shore. How the golden scales of the minnows glistened in the boats then!

On any morning, Tobe could be seen carrying his gear down the country road heading toward the lake, even before the first hint of the sun was on the horizon. Usually he was the first out on the water. He loved the cool morning air and the way sounds traveled off the water, blending with the sound of the waves on the shore. He loved to watch the dawn slowly transform his world and fill it with light.

To see other fishermen arriving on the pier always lifted Tobe's spirits. They were his friends, though they had their share of quarrels and upsets. Yet they always seemed to work them out. He fished beside them, day in and day out, from dawn and sometimes deep into night, depending on what the breezes and moon were doing. They helped each other through the hard times and the storms. All in all, he loved their company, their humor, their simple ways, and the light in their eyes, shining out from faces, well-worn from the heat of the sun, the rain, and the biting cold.

To be a fisherman was what Tobe always wanted—no closed, dank, business shop in the village for him. He wanted the wide-open spaces, with fresh breezes or ripping gales, it did not matter which. He wanted to see the freedom of birds as they soared and the procession of clouds through the day. He relished feeling his muscles throwing out the nets— the strain of drawing them in—muscles and bones lifting and pulling and lungs gasping for air. Even the inevitable cuts, sores, and exhaustion satisfied him. *Ah, to live the time of day, not by a clock but by the living pulse of nature itself!*

In the intervals between casting out his nets and pulling them in, Tobe daydreamed or drew with charcoal or pencil in his sketchbook. He would sometimes give the drawings a wash of color with a brush. He would draw a tree on the shore, a cloud, a bird in flight, a fisherman doing this or that, or just some meaningless doodle. He thought of himself as only having the most modest skill. Yet, people seemed to be more than willing to part with a few bronze ducats for one of his sketches, always to Tobe's delight and surprise.

He scampered up an embankment and turned on a trail heading east over the rolling hills that spread out from the village. The hills were lightly sprinkled with farmhouses and barns. Forests of old, majestic trees, too, populated these hills. It was said their silent thoughts fell gently on all who passed below. There were also parcels of land cleared among the forest groves, creating a patchwork quilt of meadows for grazing or fields for crops. Tobe ran up to the crest of the hill, past Aden's farm. The trail then went right by Tobe's house, a simple place.

The memory replayed in Tobe's mind of the day, a year or so ago, when Kallee and he were on a stroll, and they passed this very same house, then rundown and abandoned.

Tobe remembered Kallee looking at the old house and saying, "Wouldn't that make a cute place for someone? It just needs a little attention." She then pointed to the early morning horizon and said, "That warm blue glow; look how pretty it is. The house could be painted that color. Wouldn't it be lovely?"

Months later, Tobe did buy the house, with his adequate earnings from his fishing and a little thrown in from his sketches.

As he ran past the house, he thought about all the fixing up he still had to do inside, but it was coming along nicely. Over the months, he had cleared the land and planted a few fruit trees and flowering shrubs. On the outside of the house, he had replaced boards, filled cracks with putty, and sanded. He painted the wood what he called "warm horizon blue," often thinking of Kallee, and added white trim on the windows, doors, and scalloped edges on the eaves.

Perhaps, one day Kallee and I will live here together. He knew the place would come alive with her delicate, feminine touches. He knew she would see to it that his pictures, now carelessly tossed in a corner and tacked up on the walls, would be set into fine golden frames. She would also bring her strength and her love to turning the simple house into a nurturing, cozy home for them both. She was an exceptional woman, and Tobe knew it.

Our life could be beautiful together, if only . . . As he thought of her, his feet ran faster. She would be leaving the upper meadow any moment, herding the sheep down to her father's barn. She would not be expecting him.

Tobe came to a rock cairn marking the trail heading to Mahir's Meadow. The trail climbed; he kept his pace. Ahead he could see the towering mountain peaks forming an insurmountable wall on the northern edge of the valley. To the south, a similar mountain range ran almost parallel, creating the Valley of Salamine. To the west was the village of Soñadora, the sparkling lake, and the blackness of the Great Nothing.

He looked to the east, where a great expanse of hills and valleys extended out as far as the eye could see. Beyond that, he was told, were flatlands stretching as far as the mind could envision. From this frontier arose fearful tales of strange races of men and beasts in hostile lands. These imaginings, spun out of nothingness, kept the people of Soñadora content to stay right where they were.

Tobe thought of the small number of people who had dared to venture east—poets and madmen, mostly, along with a few courageous explorers.

"Travelers," they were called, usually in a judgmental tone, for they were looked down upon as dreamers, avoiding the real responsibilities and challenges of living in the world.

Of all the travelers, almost all turned back. The very few who did continue on and happened to return told of amazing things—unbelievable tales that stretched the imagination and lifted the spirit. Of course, most Soñadorians discounted such things as utter foolishness and gave them no more thought, preferring their dark tales of fear instead. Tobe, having grown ever practical, was skeptical too. Yet, he had enough of the child within him that he would still listen to the tales of their exploits, sometimes even more than once.

The fresh scent of evergreens, wafting down from the higher slopes, woke Tobe from his reverie. He became aware once again of the sound of his deep breathing, the swish of air in his ears, and the broken, rocky ground beneath his feet as he ran. Beyond all that, he became attuned to a growing stillness. He loved that stillness born of running. It was his doorway to a kind of peace.

Once again, his imagination carried him away. Images of Kallee, from that first day he noticed her, rose in his mind. She was in the market place, just one face lost among many. Then, suddenly, she stood out as if some celestial spotlight shone upon her. As their eyes met, he saw her blush and turn shy. (Though he would not admit it, he blushed, too, but in a deeper shade of red.) That sweet vulnerability he saw in her countenance he sensed was a wrapping to something precious in her. He was instantly drawn to her, with a force he did not know was possible.

As he ran up the path, a feeling of anxiety came over him. *Yes, our life together could be a beautiful thing, if only. . .* He was a cautious young man when it came to matters of the heart. Though he wanted to be with Kallee more than anything, he also felt he was not ready. He needed more time. *I have a lot to learn yet. I am so inconsistent . . . so incomplete. What do I have to offer anyone—much less anything beautiful and lasting?*

Soon his legs were scaling and propelling him over boulders as he made his way to Mahir's Meadow. Then, as he crested the hill, Kallee was visible on the far edge of the meadow, her back toward him, tending the sheep. The doubts of his heart scattered like startled birds. He worked his way toward her, climbing around the rocks and through the shrubs. Finally, he came to a large boulder where she had been, but she was nowhere to be seen.

As he made his way into the meadow, she leapt from the top of the boulder, grabbing Tobe around the neck, holding on tight.

Ah, Kallee! They both giggled as Tobe fell to his knees, and Kallee slid from his back to the ground. They playfully rolled in the grass, laughing.

There was a pause. The mood shifted. They leaned toward each other. Their lips, young, full, and ripe came closer and closer . . . and then touched. Exhilaration and fire coursed through them both. Their arms, their legs intertwined. Waves of love and passion flowed through their bodies—through their strong and graceful limbs and in the rhythms of their movements, expressing itself in every touch.

Tobe closed his eyes. Their bodies were pure energy, no longer solid enough to keep their selves apart. Tobe could feel the love in his heart flowing out of his chest right into Kallee. This love felt more real than any solid thing in the world. He could not tell where he ended and Kallee began.

Tobe pulled apart, just enough to look upon the beauty and wonder of Kallee's face. Their eyes looked into each other's. It was light looking upon light and love looking upon love.

Their movements began to slow, and then came to rest in a stillness of a deep serenity. They both felt it. Their faces blossomed into smiles. Their cup was full to overflowing. They were exceedingly grateful, carefree, and in love.

Tobe gently held Kallee and began to stroke her hair. The stillness of the moment enveloped them as time passed—sweet, ripe moments. Tobe could feel Kallee pressing heavier on his arm, as she started to fall asleep. A soft sigh came from her lips. Tobe felt the sun on his face; the fresh air filled his lungs. He could still feel an echo of Kallee's kiss upon his lips. An overwhelming wave of happiness welled up inside him. *Ah, the miracle of holding something so precious!* There was no place that Tobe would rather be than in the meadow with Kallee in his arms. In this moment, he did not want or need anything more from life.

Yet these moments of fullness and perfection are but fleeting things in this world, and little did Tobe suspect that, at that very moment, events were moving toward him with unstoppable resolve, rolling in with the power of a gigantic wave—a tsunami that would change his life forever. If he had known that these events were coming, he would have lost all sense of self-assurance. He would have been filled with a quaking, for it is the nature of people on the edge of the world to fear change and the unknown above all else.

CHAPTER TWO
The Gift in the Meadow

Courage is demanded of us to have strength for the strange,
singular, and most inexplicable events we may encounter.

Rainer Maria Rilke

THE DAY WAS CLEAR, the air delicate and fresh, with a gentle warmth growing upon it. To the north, about the mountain peaks, mist was collecting and turning into little clouds, pure white in the morning light. In the valley, everything was full and burgeoning with life. Spring had come to Soñadora.

Tobe's dory was already setting low in the water from his catch. He wanted to throw out the net a few more times before calling it a day, but first he longed to go to the nearby meadow—to rest and close his tired eyes for a spell. His body yearned to feel the warm, solid earth beneath his back—perhaps even to fall asleep.

He hauled the net into the boat, pouring the minnows into baskets, which he then secured. His agile yet strong, calloused hands firmly gripped the oars. He turned his dory toward the shore, and in perfect unison, the oars propelled the dory on its way with a steady rhythm. Tobe could feel the strain of his muscles as the keel sliced through the water, creating a tiny wake.

As he rowed, Tobe looked over his shoulder. A chrysalis he had found the day before hung from a branch, tied to the bow.

Tobe mused, *Do you dream in there, caterpillar? Are you awake, watching yourself dissolving? Are you afraid?*

Don't worry. One day you will come out of that darkness and find you have wings! As they stretch open, you will see how beautiful you are, and you will experience the exhilaration of flight—having only been a crawly thing before! How gracefully you will then glide on wings of . . .

Tobe paused, searching his mind for a word that meant "delicate," "paper thin," "beautifully painted in bright and iridescent colors," or a word that meant "full of strength and endurance" and "can carry one over very long distances." *Was there even such a word?* he wondered.

A refreshing breeze blew across Tobe's face, as the keel touched the shore. He sat there motionless for a moment, looking at the chrysalis. He smiled. Then all his thoughts faded. He looked around at the water, the shore, the distant mountains. All felt so perfect and complete. He savored the feeling of tranquility that swept over him. He stepped from the dory, securing it with a rope, tying it to a large branch of an old fallen tree.

Tobe left the shore and walked up a barely visible path, one made by only his own footsteps. It meandered through a few evergreen trees. Then, a sunlit meadow of wildflowers of intense color—brilliant yellow, red, and violet—spread before him. Tobe made his way to a spot that felt just right. He lay down in the warmth of the sun. When he looked up, the blue of the sky rushed in through his open eyes, filling his body, washing away the heaviness of fatigue. Instantly, he felt *a pure blue joy* filling him! Every now and then, too, a white cloud would enter his eyes and peacefully float through him, brushing his inner world with the serenity of its effortless, silent glide.

He breathed in the scent of pine, mixed with the perfume of wild flowers. He became filled with the sounds of bees humming, the soft, papery flapping of the wings of passing dragonflies, and the occasional melodious deep-throated warble of birds. His body, warmed by the gentle sun, began to melt into the earth. He grinned, slowly closing his eyes, and he watched as his world turned into the soft glow of light through closed eyelids. Everything merged into an underlying stillness. Tobe sighed and gently slipped into a deep sleep.

Then it happened. A light appeared, brighter than the sun! It slowly glided above the meadow and stopped, hovering over Tobe as he slept. The miller's daughter, the one with the mysterious yellow eyes, saw it. She was gathering healing herbs in the forest that day. She watched, standing in the shadows of the tall cedars as the light grew brighter and brighter. "*An*

Asleep in the Meadow

Arushah!" she muttered, awestruck as if in a reverent prayer. It meant "angel spirit." In the next instant, the light shot off through the sky like a shooting star.

Tobe woke with a jolt. Startled and gasping, he bolted upright. He tried to gather his senses as he looked around. Things started to come into focus. Yet, he felt peculiar. He stood. The sensation of dizziness and disorientation overwhelmed him. His lungs desperately gasped for air, but seemed to find little of it. His movements were awkward and a bit off balance, like nothing he had ever felt before. Perplexing feelings—all gray and moody—started stirring inside him. Even though his eyes were wide open, he felt like he was under the heavy spell of a troubling dream.

He was sure that fishing would clear his senses. Confused and dazed, he made his way back to the lake and his dory. His unsteady hands untied the rope. He pushed off. The awkward rocking of the dory, with a few strokes of the oars turned into a smooth, reassuring glide. But Tobe could not get rid of that foreboding feeling. His insides felt like stacked-up boxes, all askew and tottering, ready to fall at any moment.

As he fished, the wind picked up. Angry, sharp-toothed waves covered the water, turning the lake agitated and hostile. The clouds, which earlier had innocently played on the mountains to the north, merged into one huge, black cloud, now moody and heavy. It quickly spread across the whole valley, throwing everything into dark shadow. Then, the last glow of light on the distant hills went out. All the other fishermen had already gone in, knowing the storm was coming fast and sensing it would be a bad one.

Tobe did not catch a single minnow that afternoon, which had never happened before. Giving up and with a heaviness pressing down on him, he headed toward the shore. There was a sudden ear-piercing crack of thunder. Tobe jumped. A heavy steel door in his heart slammed shut, and all of the tottering boxes inside him swayed violently and came crashing down.

Tobe fought off a sense of panic as he rowed. Battling against the wind, he finally reached the dock after a fierce, exhausting struggle. He fought the storm as he tied up his dory—before the gales and waves could pull her back out to the lake to sink her.

As quickly as he could, he threw the baskets of minnows onto a handcart, as the rain slashed at his skin. He grabbed the backpack containing his sketching things, and still resisting the furious wind and his hellish inner darkness, he pushed the cart down the dock in the direction of the marketplace, relinquishing everything else in his dory to the storm.

Tobe could only make out a couple of people still scurrying about in the gloom, putting the last of their goods away. He stopped the cart at the deserted fish vendor stand, the tables boarded up like caskets. Goran, of course, was nowhere in sight. Tobe pried off the lid of the nearest long coffer. It was empty, and better yet, it still had ice. He poured in his baskets of minnows, one after another. With the rain washing down his face, Tobe struggled to get the heavy lid back on, as the wind seemed equally determined to send the lid into wild, chaotic flight.

Leaving the cart where it was, Tobe bolted off, his legs quivering. He ran like a madman, trying to escape the menacing shadows growing inside of him. He ran up the sloping lanes of the village—cold, desolate canyons, dark except for the muted lights seen through closed curtains.

Every impression of Soñadora awkwardly tumbled into him as he ran, plummeting into the utter blackness of his heart. The world was becoming an alien place. What filled Tobe with unbridled terror was that he was becoming an alien to *himself*!

As his panic rose, his pace quickened. The village gave way to barns and farmhouses, ghostly dark silhouettes standing out before the flashes of illumined sky, as distant lightning struck. He was on the path now to his home. He ran—he ran with all his might, but he could not outrun the shadows that had grabbed him with a strangling hold.

In one bound, he leaped over the steps onto the porch. The pounding of his heart and his tortured thoughts mingled with the sound of his gasping breaths and the howling of the wind, fusing into one note of chaos and misery. The storm savagely shook every living thing, as if it thirsted for its very life. A piercing, blinding flash of bright, stark light shocked Tobe's world. The sound of thunder slashed through him like a sharp, wielded ax.

He felt the cold of the metal knob as he opened the door and, utterly spent, stumbled in, slamming the door behind him, leaving the hungry, howling gale outside. Finally, he was safe, invisible to the world! He threw off his heavy outer fishing clothes and collapsed on his bed, still rain-drenched but too tired to care. The wind roared and moaned, and sharp needles of rain ferociously bit at the windowpanes as Tobe fell into a deep, deep sleep.

On the lake, Tobe's dory rocked violently back and forth, the chrysalis still holding tenaciously to the branch. Along its side, with the softest sound, a delicate tear started to appear, and then paused—revealing deep in its shadows, wings of yellow with a touch of iridescent blue.

As Tobe slept, he dreamed. Within the depths of a tranquil darkness, unrecognizable shapes began to emerge. As they drew closer, it became clear that they were toys. On and on they came, toys of all kinds: stuffed toys with glass eyes; wooden soldiers with shiny gold buttons; hand-carved puppets freshly painted; dolls all fancy with real hair, wearing pressed dresses, as well as plain simple ones with stitched eyes; and rocking horses with long, flowing manes and tails.

Off to the side, a group of toys gathered, seven in all. They made a circle, holding hands. They began moving, like a spinning wheel, dancing and singing, "We are toys. We are not real. We are toys. We are not real." On and on they danced, repeating their simple song.

"If you dance long enough," said a voice reverberating through the darkness, "you *will* become *real!*"

With a new enthusiasm, the toys continued to spin and sing. Suddenly, a dazzling light from above shone down on them, and a spiral staircase appeared, its top invisible in the light.

At that moment in the dream, Tobe became aware that he was in the circle, holding hands with two of the other toys. What he was, he was not sure, but he knew he was a mere toy. He broke away from the circle and approached the staircase. His little toy legs started to climb. When he finally reached the top, he found himself standing before a pair of large, wooden French doors with lace curtains. Above the doors in glowing red letters hovered the word: *INLĂKESH.*

He reached up and pulled on the handle. The door opened, revealing a world of warm light. A river flowed right up to the door. The leaves of the trees that lined the far side of the river shimmered in the light, as they moved with a soft breeze.

Floating on the river, like a boat, was a bed. Sitting up in the bed, leaning back on large pillows, was a *real* boy! His head slowly turned toward Tobe. Then their eyes met. *Whoosh!* In that instant, Tobe was inside the real boy, looking out of his real eyes! *Tobe had become the real boy!*

Tobe suddenly awoke. Closed curtains filtered the bright light of day into a hushed glow. The storm was gone. All was calm. Tobe lay there, bewildered and stupefied, contemplating all the extraordinary events that had occurred over the last few hours. His mind could not even begin to make sense of it all.

Without warning, the wind outside began to blow again, growing louder and louder. The windowpanes rattled. The sound scraped raw across Tobe's tired nerves. He forced himself out of bed and walked to the

The Real Boy in the Dream

window. Pulling apart the curtains, he saw the swirling cloud of leaves and twigs of a dust devil. Then the wind died; all the leaves and debris fell to the ground. Everything became still. An eerie silence settled upon the house. Tobe heard a thud on the wooden planks of the porch, followed by what sounded like slow, intentional steps. Tobe could feel his heart beating.

Cautiously, he went to the door and opened it a crack. He saw nothing. He stepped out onto the porch and looked all around, but all he saw were the rolling hills with bushes and trees washed clean from the storm. Nothing else unusual was visible. *The sound of footsteps*, he told himself, *must have been the boards settling after the wind.*

As he was going back inside, he glanced down and his attention rested on a thin package on the threshold. He stood there a moment, puzzling. Then he leaned down and picked it up. It was an ordinary-looking parcel, rectangular in shape, wrapped in a simple brown paper with twine. He took it straight to the table without bothering to close the door, and with a slash of a knife, cut the twine. His fingers tore open the paper along the folds, revealing something red.

Quickly he tore off the rest of the wrapping, exposing a book bound in red leather with gold letters glowing: *The River Is—A Poet's Journey*.

Tobe sat down. Slowly, his fingers caressed the leather, and then he opened the book. Carefully, he turned the pages, his eyes freely skimming here and there and landing for a while to read a line or a full paragraph.

The moments passed. His enthusiasm started to wane, giving way to disappointment. He began to feel that the book had nothing of real substance to offer. It was too full of suffering and darkness, which he had had enough of lately. Disenchanted, Tobe left the book where it was and got up from the table, wondering where that book could possibly have come from.

He was eager now to put his life back into some semblance of order. He would go to the lake and fish for a while; that should do it. Just then a blast of air rushed through the open door, banging it against the wall, sending the pages of the book swishing about. Tobe stood there, his gaze transfixed. As quickly as the wind started, it was over. The pages settled. Tobe could not help but lean over and look at what lay open before him. His heart stopped. There, standing out in the sea of words, in capital letters was the word: *INLĀKESH*—the word he had seen above the door in his dream.

He sat down, and with a new zeal began to peruse the book. His eyes gaily skipped about. The poet's words now held him mesmerized, filling him with new and wonderful images. The book spoke of a land of extraordinary beauty, of peculiar creatures and happenings. It spoke of a river— changeless, mysterious—called *Is* and a giant fish called *The Great Fish*.

The book kept Tobe under its spell. He gave up any idea of doing anything else that day. He was going to give this book his full attention and do nothing else. And that he did. Night came, and many hours later when night finally turned into dawn, his eyes grew too tired to read, and he made his way to bed and crawled in between the sheets. When he awoke a few hours later, he threw on his robe and went to the book, first thing. Again, he could not put it down. He read and read, taking time only to eat—and not very much at that. Day followed night, and night grew into day, again, and again.

The poet had an uncanny way of speaking to Tobe's heart. "You who feel incomplete are stronger than you think. You are more amazing than you can imagine!"

"Go to the River!" the poet kept saying. "Ride It to the center of everything!"

The book made Tobe continue to question. *Who am I? Could Inlăkesh show me?* He felt a strange stirring growing inside him. *If I would go to Inlăkesh, I would finally have something to offer to others, to Kallee, and most importantly, myself!*

No one in the village saw Tobe for days, and they grew concerned. A few were sent to check on him. Tobe answered their knocks by sticking his head out and politely thanking them for their concern. He reassured them that he was well and should be out on the lake in no time. He begged them not to worry. At that, he smiled politely, quickly shut the door, and went back to his book and his contemplations.

On and on Tobe read, stopping occasionally to write something, hoping to clarify some ponderous question, or perhaps to have an answer revealed.

Though Tobe could not wrap his mind around a lot of what the poet was saying, he sensed the truth of it. When he got to the end of the book, he would return to the beginning and start all over again. Each time he found himself at the end, he would slowly read the last words that became more and more compelling: "To read about Inlăkesh is nothing. To go there is *everything*." Each time those words went deeper, until finally he knew, beyond a doubt, that he had to go to Inlăkesh. *No matter the difficulties and hardships, I have to go. I have to see it with my own eyes! I have to find the River Is!*

He put the book down and thought about it all, hard and long, and as he thought, his eyelids grew heavy and began to close.

CHAPTER THREE
On the Road

'Tis not too late to seek a newer world.
Alfred Lord Tennyson

 T FIRST, THE LITTLE flames from the tipped-over candle were like mere children, dancing and playing upon the papers, but in no time, they grew fierce, tall, and hungry—devouring wood, cloth, and everything else. Tobe woke in a panic, with the flames roaring all about him. Frantically, he grabbed his pencils, paints, and sketchbook and threw them into his backpack. He then escaped into the cool night air.

Underneath the starry sky he stood, watching. In seconds, the flames consumed his little home. His mind was reeling. The swirling flames were like the swirling pain inside him. Amid his anguish, a calm thought came: *This is it. The time has come to begin the journey. Let's go! Could the timing be more perfect?*

Suddenly Tobe was overcome by a deep sense of loss. In the flames, he had left the poet's book. He was surprised that he felt the pain of this loss almost more deeply than the loss of his home. Then he realized that this was the way the poet would want it. *It's not about words now. It's about experience!*

Tobe walked down the path, turning his back to what remained of his home, engulfed in flames. Atop the hills, a soft, faint glow in the sky could be seen—a harbinger of the coming day. He stepped onto the dirt road, in the direction of Inlăkesh, and stopped. It seemed most odd that no one stirred and no dog barked at the flickering flames.

Mysterious things were happening, and what happened that night was strange indeed. While hard to believe, those were not real flames after all. That is the reason why no neighbors stirred, nor dogs barked. Sometimes the mind plays curious tricks. It was no natural world through which Tobe was traveling now. Each step was taking him deeper into the mind, and where the real world ended and his mind began he could no longer tell apart.

He deeply breathed in the cool air, heavy with the smell of sheep. He studied the dirt road. There were fresh tracks—and Kallee's footprints. He felt a shiver of uncertainty. Tobe followed the road until he came to the rock cairn that marked the trail. He began his ascent towards the mountains and Mahir's Meadow. His mind raced. He felt unsure how to explain it all to Kallee. *I don't even know how to explain it to myself!*

He could hear the bleating of sheep a short distance ahead, their smell grew stronger. Then he saw her, faintly in the morning light. He called out. Kallee stopped, turned, and seeing Tobe approaching, smiled.

Tobe ran up to her and took her hand, looking earnestly into her eyes. He paused. She sensed something. "What is it, Tobe?"

"Kallee . . . the house . . . is gone . . . burnt, all of it."

"Oh, Tobe, I am so sorry . . . all your work."

"I can rebuild it . . .," said Tobe, "when I return." *There, I've said it!* But he did not know how to continue.

Kallee looked puzzled. "What do you mean 'return'?"

He stood, waiting for words to come that would explain and comfort her. No words came.

Finally, "I am going on a journey," tumbled out. Tobe listened to his own words as if they were coming from a stranger . . . an inept stranger. "I have to . . ."

Kallee grew more confused. "What are you saying, Tobe? Tell me." She crossed her arms.

"It's called Inlăkesh . . . the place I'm going."

"Inlăkesh!" replied Kallee in disbelief. "My great-uncle spoke of it . . . in his bedtime stories—stories of make-believe. My dear Tobe," her face filled with concern, "what if what they say is true, and it's not a real place?"

"Oh, but it is! I know it . . . I know it in my bones." He dared not mention the poet's book. She might not understand how something as

Burning House—My Journey Begins
from Tobe's Sketchbook

simple as a book could turn his world upside down. He didn't understand it himself.

Kallee stood there silently. Tobe could see it in her eyes. It was as if she were scanning through time, desperately trying to get some clue of what was to come. "I'm worried . . . I'm scared," Kallee finally said. "Anything could happen to you out there." She stepped toward Tobe and put her arms tightly around him, burying her head in his chest. Tobe was overcome. He hugged her firmly.

"I *must* go . . ." Tobe paused, "no matter what."

"Yes, I know."

He looked deeply into Kallee's eyes. "I wish we could share the adventure together." He looked away. It was only a half-truth, for he was not certain what was to come.

"I am not brave enough for such adventures," Kallee said.

Tobe had his doubts about that. He had seen such strength and determination in her. She could be fearless.

"Besides, my father needs my help now more than ever." Kallee's eyes began to tear. She was absorbing every impression of Tobe now, as if it might be the last time she would ever see him.

Then an amused expression came to her face. With a voice that glowed with a cheeriness through the tears, she said, "My Tobe, a *'traveler'*! If anyone can make it to Inlãkesh, you can." She wiped her tears.

She affectionately gave Tobe a little kiss, smiling. He could taste her tears and feel the heat coming from her cheeks. Tobe could see there was a light in her eyes.

Kallee's words now flowed calmly, rising from some deep center within her. "Oh, Tobe . . . my dearest friend . . . my love, I will miss you so very, very much. I want for you what will bring you happiness." Kallee let go of Tobe and turned away. "But this pain . . . it is unbearable. I don't know how I can live with *it* . . . and live without *you*."

Tobe reached out and touched Kallee. "I love you." Until now, he had no idea of the depth of those words. In that moment, love was all he felt.

Kallee turned toward Tobe. They hugged each other—stronger this time. Tobe felt his resolve melting. Before it was too late, he broke free from Kallee. He turned and walked back down the trail. He had never known such heartbreaking pain!

"I will wait for you!" Kallee's voice rang clear, through the distance. "Take care, my Love!"

Tobe waved, smiling through the heartache, yet comforted by her words. He continued his descent.

He made his way back to the road and looked toward the east. The road meandered off into the distance in the early light. He had traveled this part of the valley many times before. Yet he knew that in a few days he would be where few in his village had ever gone. Though he felt the pull in his heart for all he was leaving behind, he rejoiced in the sense of adventure and the open road that lay before him. He had never known such freedom before.

The dawn broke. The road changed from dirt to large, flat stones, which spoke hauntingly of an industrious people long forgotten. The road was host to an assortment of weeds stubbornly growing between the tightly fitting rocks, unhampered by the travel of people.

Tobe hiked up and down, over hill and valley, through forests and glens. He finally came to the point where everything was unfamiliar. He looked back in the direction of Soñadora, which was now invisible in the distance, and then turned toward where he was heading, into the unknown. He felt his confidence slide out of him with a slight chill, and in crept a feeling of vulnerability. Tobe accepted this vulnerability as his new traveling companion and continued on.

Meadows thick with grass gave way to a drier land, and the forests dwindled to an occasional solitary tree. An arid landscape stretched out before him, with large boulders scattered about. When the stone road ended, Tobe followed a path a short distance away, made by wild animals—he assumed.

Tobe was ready for a rest. The path led to a large tree ahead, offering good shade. *A perfect place.* Just then, he heard the sound of steps coming from behind. He turned. Another person was walking quickly, still a distance away, coming closer. The man did not slow as he passed. He glanced at Tobe saying, "The carnival is here!"

Then the strangest thing happened. In an instant, the clothes and skin of the man became transparent, and then disappeared completely, revealing cogs, gears, and wires. Little sparks were shooting off here and there. He moved smoothly, without a skip, clink, or flaw. His eyes, set in sockets, turned this way and that by what looked like little rubber bands. He was constructed so perfectly in every way!

Tobe was flabbergasted. *Are those eyes of glass or are they real? Do they really see? And how is it possible that something so mechanical could have a voice and movements so lifelike?*

"Where are you from? Who made *you*?" Tobe shouted at the mechanical man as he continued down the path.

"Who made you?" the mechanical man shouted back in jest, over his shoulder. Then he was gone as quickly as he had appeared.

All this would have given Tobe much to think about, except he had no time for that. Something else caught his eye. At first, it appeared as a shadow of something, but then, Tobe realized, there was no "something." The shadow began to move, quietly gliding across the surface of the ground, coming quicker and straight for him!

Poor Tobe, he was completely helpless. The shadow rushed up to him and stopped. Shocked, Tobe lost his balance and tumbled in. He screamed in horror as he fell and fell. He fell through dismal, dreary feelings, all slithering upon each other, creating all kinds of frightening images in Tobe's mind and waves of nausea in his guts and heart. Tobe was in sheer panic. He felt as though, in that one, dark hole, there was as much darkness as in the whole night sky. He had no idea how his falling would end, or if it ever would.

How long he fell, Tobe could not tell. Nevertheless, time did pass. And without knowing how, Tobe rose up from so far down, to find himself standing once again on what felt like solid ground. He looked around. The dark hole was nowhere to be seen. It seemed a wonder that he could stand clear headed and secure, once again in his skin.

What was that?! He stood there exhausted, still reeling.

Tobe decided not to stay a moment longer. He headed down the path, in the same direction as the mechanical man. Then to his horror, he saw another dark hole quickly approaching. That there could be another loathsome dark hole was inconceivable. (Yet Tobe would come to find out that there were as many dark holes as there were dark thoughts in his head.) Then, just as before, he found himself falling, falling into another hole.

By the end of the day (or perhaps many days?), Tobe had lost count of the dark holes into which he had fallen—and his journey had just begun! He started to question if there were not a better way to get to Inlåkesh. For the first time, too, he had doubts. *Perhaps it was a mistake to leave Kallee and the village. What if they are right, and Inlåkesh doesn't even exist? Look at me: I am nothing exceptional to go on such an adventure. What was I thinking? What am I doing out here, in who knows where? This is madness, and I am the maddest of all.* Then suddenly, he realized that once again he was falling, falling through the thoughts and feelings of another dark hole!

Tobe began to perceive that there were different kinds of dark holes. Some were small and seemed innocent, no larger than a flower, but as he stepped, they would instantly open up, becoming large enough to swallow him whole. Others were big—big enough for elephants to fall into, and still he had a hard time avoiding them.

Tobe learned to keep an eye out for the holes. Some holes, if he waited for the right second to step aside, would zoom harmlessly by. Some were shy, and if he kept looking at them, they would scurry away. Some holes were particularly full of tricks and mischief. Some annoying ones would linger around, waiting for a moment of inattention on Tobe's part. Around those clever ones, he had to be particularly vigilant. Nevertheless, with some wit and a bit of skill, Tobe did get better at avoiding them.

Tobe also discovered that when he did find himself falling into a dark hole, he was not totally helpless. His attitude determined everything. The more fearful he was, the faster and further he fell. Yet if he were able to accept his predicament, the falling would start to slow, turning into a gentle glide. The slower he fell, the more clearly he could see the wretched thoughts, feelings, and images he was falling through. Seeing them more

I discovered going down is just a part of going up.

One does get better at this whole dark hole mess.

Rhapsody of Dark Holes in G Minor
from Tobe's Sketchbook

clearly, he found that they were not as frightening as he imagined. They had no power to hurt that *he* did not give them. Seeing this, Tobe observed the darkness gradually fade into light.

He learned that no matter how dark the hole or how far he fell, eventually he *would* end up on solid ground again. This gave him such confidence. So it was that Tobe began to tame the dark holes, and they bothered him less and less.

The trail twisted and turned, so that Tobe was no longer sure in which direction he was heading. The distant mountain peaks appeared sinister and foreboding. The black clouds that encircled them shot off bolts of lightning, and thunder rumbled across the plain. The moon, almost full, was like a ghost haunting day. Large eroded shapes stood across the landscape—eerie, haunting figures. The land, tortured by the sun and the lack of rain, was no more than a desert. Anything living gasped for moisture. Through the day, Tobe watched as clouds would come and tease—holding out their promise of rain—only to melt away again, without one gift of a drop.

He heard a noise far away. *Something is approaching!* The muffled sound of voices was coming closer. Cautiously, he made his way behind a rock, where he could safely crouch, unseen. From there he had a good vantage point. Below was a clearing, with a slight rise beyond.

Over the rise, they started to come: creatures that looked like Tobe in every way, except they had transparent bubbles over their heads. The spheres went down to their shoulders. "Bubble People," Tobe coined them, and he liked the name for it suited them well. Carrying baskets, they started to appear, one after another, traveling in Tobe's direction. He counted about twenty or more. They stopped in the clearing, put down their baskets, and began picking up what looked like absolutely nothing from the ground, carefully placing whatever "it" was in their baskets. They worked their way across the clearing, their baskets, seemingly, becoming heavier as they went. Tobe watched as they fought each other over what they had gathered.

Their bubbles appeared smudged and scratched from use. Some were thicker than others. The children's bubbles were thinner, clearer, and not as perfectly formed. The youngest ones had only a faint wisp of one, like a clear vapor. Only the infants were completely free of a bubble altogether.

Tobe observed that these Bubble People seemed to be prone to strange fits of behavior, swinging wildly from happiness to despair, from kindness to destructive rage. He observed that what seemed to make them act so erratically were all sorts of images that filled their bubbles.

These images were like dreams that they watched with their eyes open, as if in a trance. Some of the images were of themselves, and some were images of others. Some of these images were fearful; some were of revenge and attack; some of hurts and injustices. Pains and anxieties of all kinds filled their bubbles. Pleasant images also existed—happy ones of friendship, romance, and pleasures. These clouded their spheres almost as much, if not more.

At other times, an emotional fog would also fill their bubbles, blending with the images and making it nearly impossible for them to see out at all. The fog came in different colors: ornery oranges and raging reds, as well as forlorn and cheerless browns, despondent grays, and doleful blues.

Tobe observed that when the Bubble People got excited about something, which happened quite often, their spheres would both fog up and fill with images, all spinning like crazy. They seemed to like getting upset or excited about things. Then, how they would fight!

They seemed to be constantly talking—mostly to themselves, their voices muffled inside their bubbles. When, however, they *did* communicate with each other, from what Tobe could tell, often no one was really listening. Particularly odd was that whenever one was speaking to another, images would appear in their bubbles of who they thought the other person was. However, Tobe noticed that in no way did the image resemble the person to whom they were speaking.

How those poor creatures did sweat and fret inside their bubbles, stumbling and fumbling about! Tobe felt sorry for them. They were alone, cut off from each other and from their world. A couple of times, Tobe thought he heard one of them sobbing in their bubble as it all became too much for them.

The thought crossed Tobe's mind that they would surely know if the trail was heading in the direction of Inlăkesh. He gathered his courage and walked down to them. Startled, all of the Bubble People stopped and looked anxiously at Tobe as he approached. He tried to reassure them of his good intentions with a smile and a gesture to shake hands—which had no effect. They studied Tobe closely, with perplexed looks. A couple of them started to feel with their hands around Tobe's head, no doubt feeling for a bubble. Tobe's unease was growing.

"Does this trail lead to Inlăkesh?" Tobe asked.

The Bubble People turned and looked at each other with puzzled expressions, mumbling to each other through their bubbles. Tobe could not make out what they were saying, but he could tell by their confused demeanors that they had no clue about what he asked.

While all this was going on, Tobe noticed a younger one of the clan, standing behind the others. At that very moment, his bubble was clearing of all haze and images. The youth suddenly found himself looking out of a clear bubble at a clean, new world! He appeared startled. His eyes were big and his mouth agape.

For a second, his eyes met Tobe's. The youth did not seem to know what to do. Tobe could see him growing uneasy and unsure of himself. His "new" bright world was becoming too much. Tobe could see a wave of fear overtake him. Instantly, the fog and images came streaming back, filling his bubble. The youth breathed a deep sigh of relief, as he returned to his old, familiar world.

"Wooph phoot toom pooh!" The words, muffled yet fervent, drew Tobe's attention. He turned. What appeared to be the leader was standing inches away from Tobe, waving his hands, shrugging his shoulders, and shaking his head excitedly as he spoke. Tobe had no idea what he was saying or why he was so upset. It was clear that there were no answers here. The leader gave Tobe a long, sideways look, and walked away. The others immediately followed, gathering up their heavy baskets and balancing them on their heads. Off they went, back in the direction from which they came.

Not having learned whether he was heading the right way, Tobe went back to the trail and continued the journey in the direction in which he had been going. By now, the day was getting on, and Tobe calculated that he couldn't have gone too far. The dark holes had distracted him, causing him to lose all sense of time.

The landscape hardly changed through the day, showing him only its tortured face beyond every rise. Finally, the intense heat of day gave way to soothing dusk. Tobe was all too glad to stop. He found a gnarled specimen of a tree standing alone. Even though it had only the most modest foliage, it gave Tobe a sense of comfort to find a living thing with which to share the coming night. From his backpack, he pulled out an apple, plucked from his uncle's orchard, some honey, and a part of a loaf of seeded bread, a gift from his neighbor, Alanah. She had no way of knowing how priceless her kind gift would become.

After eating, he gathered up some fallen branches and made a fire. He took out a shirt from the bottom of the backpack, one he wore on the lake on cool days. Its mere touch took him back to the lake and its smells. He could feel, for a moment, the ground sway as if he were once again in his dory. He placed the shirt in the saddle of a root at the base of the tree. It held his head in comfort, like an open hand. Feeling drained from the events of the day, he stretched out with a sigh. He suddenly realized how utterly tired he was. He closed his eyes, and before he knew it, fell into a deep sleep, as the last of the sun slipped slowly below the horizon.

Tobe awoke to the light of day glowing brightly about him. For breakfast, he found what he could in his backpack—another apple, some toasted grains, and a bag of nuts.

The trail was right where he left it, and for that, in this strange land, he was exceedingly grateful. Continuing the journey, he tried not to think about the uncertainties that lay ahead, determining instead to hold on to the simplicity of the moment. He passed his day, focusing intently on whatever was before him as he walked—a sparkling rock, a little desert plant, or a scurrying lizard. He found, too, that if he could stay focused like that, the dark holes were less likely to come and swallow him whole again.

CHAPTER FOUR
The Carnival

A fool sees not the same tree that a wise man sees.
William Blake

Open your eyes!
Leonardo da Vinci

ALL THAT REMAINED OF the day was a peach glow on the horizon. The first stars began to reveal themselves. Weary of the terrain, which was repeating itself with a stubborn monotony, Tobe crested a hill, and then stopped in his tracks. Stretching out below were hundreds of tents and booths, all lit up, with pennants flying. The hum and activity of people filled the place. Excitement was everywhere! A huge banner near the entrance read: "The Fantastic Carnival Phantasmagoria!"

Beyond the entrance was a wide walkway, lined on both sides with tents and booths packed closely together. In the distance, a multitude of carnival rides were visible, all decorated in lights, rising and spinning against the early evening sky. From this center, aisles of tents radiated out in all directions, like spokes on a wheel. Whistling fireworks shot overhead, and with a soft puff, exploded into colorful, brilliant bursts of sparkling light, filling the sky.

Tobe did not hesitate. He dashed down the hill toward the entrance. The noise was deafening. People were streaming in from all directions, jostling and pressing him along.

People paused to read large billboards of posted notices. In big red letters were the words: "Warning," "Beware," "Danger," and "Not Liable." Tobe's eyes quickly glanced over the many pages of rules and a list of the things for which the carnival was not legally responsible—all in that strange language lawyers speak. A few words popped out: "Grave bodily harm and death . . . tornadoes . . . floods . . . lightning strikes . . . famines . . . run over by a train . . . or choke on a piece of meat." Also on the list were social catastrophes: "wars, revolutions, bombings, lootings, murders, abuse . . . and attacks of all sorts." And at the very bottom was typed, "Thank you, and have a nice day!" Tobe was determined to enter.

From behind him, Tobe heard: "Some say that subconsciously we choose all that happens to us: tsunamis, earthquakes, attacks, and all. Yet, it's odd—we are not conscious of it. We have no idea what we've chosen . . . or when it will happen, so it's like a surprise. Weird, isn't it?"

Tobe turned to see who was speaking to him and was stunned to see the person that he had seen on the trail, the one who had turned into the mechanical man. The man looked at Tobe with a puzzled expression saying, "I know you, don't I? Yes, you are the fellow I saw in the desert. My name is Sebastian." He extended his hand. "I'm glad you could make it."

"My name is Tobe." They shook hands. Sebastian's hand felt real enough.

Tobe looked over Sebastian closely. He saw no signs of gears or wires anywhere. Sebastian was fairly thin, wearing glasses, probably no more than thirty years of age. He was a few inches taller than Tobe, a bit intellectual-looking and ungainly, but steady.

"It makes no sense," Tobe said, responding to Sebastian's earlier comment. "Why would we choose such things to happen to us? We would have to be *insane*."

Sebastian shrugged, "Who says we're not. If you don't like that theory, there are others: like karma—what you give out comes back. Or there is the old angry-God idea . . . but the God I know is *nothing* like that. We'll let the philosophers figure it all out. What do you say?" said Sebastian, glancing toward the entrance. "Let's go and have a good time!"

As they turned to go, something on the billboard caught Tobe's eye. "Look! We're supposed to choose a costume and a role to play while we are here at the carnival."

The range of choices fascinated Tobe. One could be anything one wanted: a singer; a princess, a servant, or a ruler of men; a priest or a beauty queen; a racer, an inventor, or a builder of things; a person of great accomplishment, or one who simply does nothing at all. On and on the choices went.

Tobe perused the list carefully, and finally picked the role of the "traveling poet." He felt that it fit him best, since the role of a "traveling fisherman who sometimes draws" wasn't anywhere on the list.

Tobe liked the role of a poet, too, because the power of words to create their magical effects had always intrigued him. *A good "word trainer,"* Tobe surmised, *can take even a small four-legged word and make it jump through hoops, all ablaze, or can dress up the word in tights and make it do summersaults and handstands in the heart of a reader, bringing the reader to applause . . . or tears.* Such was the power of words—and Tobe wanted to learn all about that!

Just then, the surge of the crowd swept up Tobe and Sebastian, and pushed them through the gate.

"You know, when I saw you in the desert," said Tobe, loudly above the din, "it was the oddest thing. For a moment, you appeared like . . . like a machine, with levers, gears, and wires. It was amazing!"

Tobe paused, and then asked what was really on his mind. "Are you real or are you a . . .?"

Sebastian chuckled and looked at Tobe curiously, "I can assure you: I'm as *real* as you are . . . whatever that might mean."

They came to a large tent with a sign that read: "Costumes for Role Town." Here were racks of costumes of every imaginable sort. There were uniforms for majorettes, housekeepers, beekeepers, bellhops, and chauffeurs; overalls for carpenters, firemen, and farmers; smocks for artists, cooks, nurses, and patients; sports apparel for ball players, bull fighters, joggers, jousters, bungee jumpers, and bicycle riders; robes for priests, judges, boxers, and kings; suits for lawyers, politicians, and even hooligans, too. For those ladies that wished, they could also choose ballroom dresses, dinner dresses, suit dresses, baby doll dresses, wrap dresses, sun dresses, and pinafores—in all shades of colors, and fabrics of lace, silk, or plain soft cotton.

Tobe was already dressed as a traveling poet, but he thought that a hat with a little flair would set off the image with a perfect touch. He picked a felt fedora and bent the brim up just right. Sebastian chose the role of "professor." He picked out a simple tweed coat, a lightly pressed shirt, a pipe, and wing-tip shoes. Tobe talked him into getting a hat just like his—just for fun.

Tobe and Sebastian then walked down one of the main aisles, amazed at the spectacle. Jugglers, clowns, and magicians, all in colorful costumes, strolled about as they performed. The crowd was in a festive mood. Everything was in abundance. Booths were selling a cornucopia of things to eat and entertain, displaying a multitude of glittering trinkets to catch the eye. Experiences and pleasures were readily available to satisfy any taste. Anything you could imagine was for sale. Everywhere Tobe looked, something called to him. Everything had a price: "the price you pay . . . and then the price you pay."

Tobe ended up spending many hours at booths that tested his strength and skill. He would compete as the crowd applauded and cheered him on. How he loved their attention and praise. "What a great place!" he exclaimed.

Tobe and Sebastian made their way to "Role Town." It looked like a real town with streets, homes, restaurants, and shops, where people could act out their roles. They were called "dream roles" because they were only make-believe. A hot dog vendor stood on the street corner; a merchant was sweeping outside his shop. Through windows, Tobe could see a baker busy before his ovens, a seamstress altering hems. In the music store, instruments were being played, traded, and sold.

There were also fancy amusement park rides, including excursions into jungles. You could be an explorer, a hunter—and if you weren't careful, you could even be eaten by a tiger or a crocodile.

People with more rebellious natures could act out crimes, such as rob a bank or accost someone and steal them blind. (Tobe wondered if "the victim" was a dream role too.) All this misbehaving gave those who took a fancy to enforcing the law something to do: the policeman, the detective, the judge, and the jailer.

Tobe and Sebastian were drawn to the cafés, where they found other artists, writers, and "intellectuals" (which Tobe, before long, surmised could mean almost anything). Sebastian, the professor, fit right in. He had a flare for being able to speak to anyone about the loftiest things. His sentences, exuding an air of scholarly sophistication, flowed all wordy and in quick succession, piling high atop each other—growing like the great tower of Babel. Cleverly, he always changed the subject before the whole thing could come toppling down. Tobe marveled at the mind's ability to spin endless, intricate prattle out of itself.

It was in a café that Tobe wrote his first poem:

Carnival I

Carefree Carnival Days

What a delightful place to come and play
    Through the night and
        through the day.

The cup overflows
    as life goes
        on its merry way.

Let's just have fun while we are here.
    Come, sit, my friend, have another beer!

Why not taste all your pleasures
    to their full measures?

Cast all your cares away,
    for this is a brand new day,
        And there is, after all,
            No real penalty to pay!

Tobe was quite pleased with his new creation. He confidently presented his first poem to those gathered in the café. Unfortunately, his poem was only met with snickers and condescending comments.

"It's too sweet," said one.

"It's too shallow," said another.

"Make your poems *bleed*, young lad."

"It has no rhythm to its step; it has no meter. It is but fumbling about."

"You write like a child, man," said one. "You know nothing of the craft of the poet's art, and it's clear you lack the poet's eye or the poet's heart."

Tobe felt small . . . and he was growing smaller with the increasing pain of his self-conscious blush.

Oh, what I would give to be out on the water in my boat this moment, to feel my fishing net in my fingers. Now that I know how to do. . .and do well!

Despite his companions' obvious lack of appreciation, Tobe quickly recovered, and true to his character, he decided he would not give up . . . at least not yet.

At the same time, people had gathered around and with much curiosity and appreciation, were looking at Tobe's sketchbook. His drawings and paintings created very definite effects on all who looked upon them. So it was not long before he found himself warmly accepted into their eclectic, eccentric, little unorthodox club. For this, Tobe was surprised and very grateful.

Time slipped away. Night turned into day and day into night, again and again. One day, as Tobe looked around Role Town, it became clear to him that everyone was deep into his or her own role. They had forgotten that the roles were but part of a game they were playing. Tobe could see that, for many people, their roles had become burdens—empty and futile. Their roles no longer brought happiness or pleasure. Yet, they could not lay them down. Tobe did not realize it, but he, *too*, had forgotten it was but a game he played.

Eventually, though, Tobe did start losing interest in Role Town. The idea of exploring the rest of the carnival began to seem fresh and exciting again. He was ready for a new adventure. Sebastian agreed. It was time to move on.

As soon as they stepped out of the gate of Role Town, Sebastian came to a sudden stop and stood there staring.

"Do you see that?!" said Sebastian. He could not contain his excitement. "Come on, Tobe!" Sebastian started walking quickly down the lane lined with booths and tents.

Tobe looked to see what had captivated Sebastian. Just a little ways up the lane was a large tent decorated with red and pink hearts, and with heart-shaped balloons swaying in the breeze. A huge sign read, "The Love Tent." It was the largest sign that Tobe had seen in the carnival so far. Beneath it were other smaller signs in lights, which read, "Find Your Soulmate," "Romance," "Eternal Love," "Bliss."

Tobe hurried to keep up with Sebastian. But as he went his feet seemed to grow heavier—his thoughts returning home to Kallee. His heart ached; *she* was all he wanted.

"Let's find us a good woman," Sebastian called back, "someone to hold us tight in the night!" Over his shoulder Sebastian threw Tobe a glance with a wink. "You know you're lonely. Hurry up!"

Tobe said nothing but hurried to catch up. Yes, he *did* feel his loneliness, but there was only one he longed for.

They approached the tent and joined the crowd to get in. They stepped up and through the entrance—a large heart, big enough to walk through. The space inside was jam-packed with people. Welcoming colored lights shone around the tent. Musicians played romantic melodies as a singer sang love songs. There were shelves and shelves of items for purchase:

flowers in bouquets, row upon row of boxes of chocolates and other gifts, along with cards to express every kind of amorous sentiment. Hundreds of heart-shaped balloons of silver and red had floated up to the top of the tent with their ribbons hanging down. The tent was brimming over with the buzzing, babbling sound of excited voices.

All around were signs that read "Love & Happiness!" "Sweet Kisses," "Warm Embrace." The word "Love" was everywhere. Tobe thought longingly of Kallee.

A person came up to Sebastian and Tobe and offered to find them the "perfect match," for a fee. Of course, Tobe had no interest and Sebastian said "No, thanks," preferring the adventure of finding his own.

They spied an empty table at the back of the tent. Making their way there, they sat down and watched.

A great mixture of people filled the tent. There were people of all shapes and sizes: the very thin to the very obese, the small to the tall, the extremely beautiful to the most unattractive, the young to the very old. There was every shade of skin and disposition; males and females, switching and playing different roles in every possible combination. Anyone could "love" anyone, and often did.

People were strolling about or sitting at tables. Everyone was busy checking out each other. It was odd to Tobe how people were strutting around, using their charms to allure. Their lure was their bodies, the sparkle in their eyes, their enticing smiles, and amiable countenance—often cleverly manipulated for their purpose—or so Tobe suspected. There were also others who were "selling" their story, or their personalities—being witty or refined—using them to catch their "catch." It all made Tobe think of being out on his boat and catching minnows with his net.

"Do you feel the pull of love?" asked Sebastian. "There's no greater force!"

"Is it 'love' we see?" Tobe replied. "We are easily deluded."

"You are a touch cynical today, Mr. Tobe."

Tobe responded with a shrug of his shoulders, and then added, "Just look. See how people here are *consumed* by this search for 'love' . . . as if they desperately need something outside of them to complete themselves."

"Yes, what about you—you and Kallee?" questioned Sebastian.

Tobe had no answer. Yet, it did make him think.

A pretty woman walked by. Sebastian became distracted. "I would sure love to lay down in that 'field,'" he said with a sigh.

Yes, she was pretty, Tobe observed. Then he saw that the room was *full* of attractive, lovely people. There was no shortage of them.

He then saw a sign in large letters, "The Honeymoon Room." It made him pause. He had heard of the "honeymoon,"—a strange thing that happens to people who "fall in love." Tobe had heard of the honeymoon's power and how it did not last. He started to suspect there was more to this tent.

Sebastian saw another "sweet thing" walking by, and this time he could not help himself. He was up in a flash before Tobe knew it. In no time, Sebastian was sitting with her at a table in a dark corner. They were animated and appeared deeply engrossed in each other. Tobe could see Sebastian putting on all his charm.

Then Tobe noticed a slit in the fabric on the far side of the tent with another sign above that simply said, "The Passing of Time." Beneath that were other signs:

"The Pain of Working It Out," "It's Not So Easy," and "Not What You Thought." These signs were much smaller, as if not to distract from the charm and appeal of the Honeymoon Room.

Tobe got up, his curiosity burning, and made his way to the opening. He stepped through and entered a much darker space. It was even more crowded than the other room. Tobe found a table where he could easily observe, and sat down. This room was not festive, nor gaily lit. Here there was a palpable difference in the air; the mood was colder. It gave Tobe a chill. He instantly could feel the thread of love between most of the couples here had grown very thin or had completely worn out.

As Tobe watched he saw that some of the most passionate couples he had seen in the Honeymoon Room barely made it into this space before they separated. The chaos of emotions was apparent here, with intimacy and commitment mysteriously evaporating away before many of the couple's eyes, sometimes to their deepest distress. They appeared powerless before this fading. What added to the chaos was that the "love" the couples shared for each other could, at any moment, lift off and fly away without any warning—often landing with another. And then what heartache! *How quickly faith falls into faithlessness, and heartache flows like a river here.*

Tobe noticed there were also different kinds of couples here. Some appeared to be no more than friends—cool and calm. *Is 'love' there, too?*

Some relationships had so little love to them that Tobe wondered why they were together at all. They looked in opposite directions as they strolled about or sat. They spoke seldom. Others were cantankerous and argued all the time. *What bonds like ropes keep these two "boxers" together, fighting so?*

He observed pairs that hung tenaciously to each other. They spoke of "commitment" and "loyalty." Tobe wondered if it was not so much about love but that they lacked the will or courage to stand alone.

He watched others who collected "intimate" relationships like trophies, putting them on some inner mantle in praise of themselves.

Then Tobe's heart lifted as his eyes fell upon an elderly couple walking hand-in-hand. They looked upon each other with such caring affection. The warmth of their sweetness toward each other flowed into Tobe, giving him new hope.

Maybe there are more like them, Tobe reassured himself. He looked around. Yes, there were. Sprinkled here and there were a few couples that actually seemed to be happy and in "love." Though when Tobe studied them more closely, he could see that in some cases this was true, but in others, there was only an imitation of happiness and love—a mere facade for show.

One thing became clear to Tobe: not one relationship he saw was a constant thing. They were always shifting about, and some wildly.

Tobe had a thought that if he wrote a poem, he might start to understand it all a bit better. He took out a folded paper and pencil and began to write:

Love

Why do I still feel as a stranger in Your house?
    A foreigner—lacking any strength to hold You and make You mine.
You are too airy and fleeting for our mortal fingers to grasp.
    You fly with a power that eclipses our mere mortal will to tame you.

Yes, You will come and sit and visit for a spell—
    Your mysterious force moving us—overwhelming us
        While you hide behind Your veil.

And then You fly off, abandoning us again,
    To our little hearts and selves

And we fall back again into darkness
    And into the empty corridors of our hearts
        Where the steps of those we once loved
            Can be heard echoing, as they depart.

"Ah, there you are!" Sebastian's voice startled Tobe.

Tobe put the pencil down, relieved of the burden of trying to write something insightful and true about love—much less with a poet's form.

"What do we have here?" Sebastian picked up the paper. He quickly glanced at it. "You wrote this?"

"Yes," replied Tobe, as if he were admitting to a crime.

"It's not bad . . . really. You may make a poet yet."

Tobe took it as a compliment, for he thought that it might be the closest he would ever come to receiving a real one.

"What happened with your woman?" asked Tobe.

"I'd rather not talk about it," said Sebastian. But then, he continued, "I thought things were going great, when all of a sudden she turned cold. Then I saw her looking at some other guy. I guess I wasn't the right kind—size, shape, or who knows. Or maybe it was just 'me.' If it was, I have no idea how to fix that! What is this chemistry stuff between people about, anyway?"

"I haven't the slightest," replied Tobe. "Attraction has a mind of its own, that's for sure," He didn't know what words to say to cheer up Sebastian. "But a lot of things have to be just right."

"From the outside," said Sebastian, "this tent sure seemed inviting. Its reality, though, is something else . . . what pain and disappointment!"

"Is there anything more confusing and difficult," said Tobe thoughtfully, "than this curious thing we call 'love'? From what I have seen so far, nothing in this whole carnival seems to drive people madder."

"It gets complicated, too," added Sebastian, "because of the darkness in ourselves. What we do to those we want to 'love'! I feel sorry for them. I should have a sign that says, 'Beware! Stay Away!' 'Danger!' 'Save Yourself the Misery!' But I am too selfish. I need others for my own pleasure, my own needs . . . especially to keep me from feeling lonely."

Tobe interjected, "But *why* is the carnival so *odd*? *Why* doesn't love flow freely here? Shouldn't it? There's something very wrong here."

"I feel we're missing a piece to this picture," added Sebastian. "Let's go before I go crazy trying to figure this all out."

They both got up from the table, put on their felt fedoras, and stepped out into the fading light of day. Both breathed out a sigh, relieved to get out of there. Things seemed refreshingly simple again in the early evening air. Yet, as they walked, they could not quite shake the shadow lingering in their hearts.

Ahead they saw a large tent packed with people. Colored lights were flashing; sounds were dinging and clanging. Signs read, "Money $$$!" "Get

Rich!" "Make a Fortune!" Inside the tent, people were putting coins into machines, or gathering around tables, playing games of chance with dice and cards. Everyone was welcome.

People also gambled at computers, betting on stocks, deeply engrossed, some nervous, some upset, their life's worth rising and falling with a line. At larger, fancy tables, people in the finest attire played games of high finance. Not everyone was welcome there. Lawyers, with briefcases in hand, gathered around these tables. The law had to be interpreted—and manipulated too. Bankers and power brokers moved pieces on a board, determining the fate of commodities, stocks, companies, financial empires, and even nations—puppet masters pulling strings.

"Same old story," muttered Sebastian.

At most of the tables, what one gained was at the expense of others who willingly came to play. But, at the high-finance tables, unsuspecting victims were the ones that were often "fleeced." This was a most peculiar, self-centered game. Greed was heavy in the air. Tobe felt sorry for many there—for what they lost in what they gained.

"Insane, isn't it?" said Sebastian. "People with so much, desperately needing more."

Inspiration touched Tobe again, and he scribbled another poem.

Piles High

O money—
    the love of you,
        though makes cents,
    makes no sense!

Security lives
    somewhere else . . .
        happiness too.

Greed's focus is future tense.
    And in the present,
        counts its present$—
        never enough—
    piles, piled high.

Is that your joy I see,
    way up at the very top

of these stacked up coins?
I think not!

Tobe studied the poem and smiled. "I've got it! I have found 'my voice'!" He excitedly handed the poem to Sebastian.

Sebastian perused it and handed it back, saying, "Best stick with drawing. Besides, Tobe, we're taking it all too seriously! We just need to relax and have some fun." Sebastian held out some money, "Here, go and place a bet."

"No thanks."

Tobe turned and headed out. Sebastian hurried to catch up. "We'll have to come back," said Sebastian. "I've got a scheme that will make us super rich!"

Outside the tent was a pile of dirty torn rags. A thin, trembling hand protruded, and a weak voice pleaded, "A few spare coins."

Sebastian leaned over and asked, "What did you choose in this, my friend? And *why*? Are you a helpless victim, or paying off a debt? Is your God angry with you, my friend?"

Tobe was growing uncomfortable.

Sebastian continued, "Or did you wish this on yourself—the fruit of some self-destructive guilt and loathing?"

There came no reply.

Tobe touched Sebastian's arm. "Come on, let's go." As they moved on, Tobe dropped a few coins into the hand, unable to give what was truly needed.

Down the next aisle, in a tent decorated in colored flags and banners, a man was standing on a raised podium and shouting. He was excited, pounding his fists, forehead wrinkled, with veins popping out. One could see the angst in his eyes.

Waving their signs and little flags, the crowd had caught his hysteria. The speaker pointed across the aisle at a different booth, decorated with the same colored banners and flags, where another man was speaking just as excitedly. He was pointing his finger angrily back across the aisle in the direction of the other speaker. He, too, had a crowd, and they, too, were all agitated. Both crowds were certain beyond a doubt that *they* were right!

The ruckus was deafening. Sometimes the two speakers were even saying the exact same thing, pointing their fingers furiously at each other. Every now and then, words broke through. Tobe heard, "Apathy will kill you . . . prevent this evil . . . if you do nothing . . . be destroyed . . . the end . . . complete destruction . . . act now . . . OR ELSE!" On and on it went.

Tobe found himself pulled in, with Sebastian by his side. When the crowd marched off, agitated and upset, to protest something or other, Tobe and Sebastian were right in the midst of it. As they marched along, Tobe suddenly realized this was not what he came to the carnival for. He stopped as the crowd marched on.

"Do some good," Tobe called out, as he watched the crowd disappear around the corner, with Sebastian lost in their midst. *I am here to catch a different kind of fish.*

Suddenly, everything was quiet as Tobe stood there. *Now, what am I doing here, anyway?* But before his mind could even think of the answer, his attention was drawn to some flashing signs where a good-sized crowd was gathered. Nearly all were men, loud and tipsy, spilling their beer as they tottered and joked.

Big, red, neon letters flashed, "DANCING GIRLS" and beneath that, "Girls! Girls! Girls!" On a stage, dancing in tiny dresses, there they were, kicking up their shapely legs, and bending this way and that. As Tobe approached, their beauty caught him off guard and took his breath away. Every curve of their bodies called to him. They were *perfect*—a pure pleasure to look upon!

Tobe began to feel uneasy, though. Something beyond his control was gaining influence over *him*. He looked around. Seductively, with ease, the dancing girls were ensnaring the men in their powerful spell. The men were *willingly* surrendering to the girls' power. The girls were "divine creatures" in the flesh! And the men were worshipping them—every inch of them—at this holy altar.

Tobe was determined to resist the spell of the girls. As he stood there, watching, he noticed one dancer in particular—the little one on the end with long, silky, amber hair. But her every move, every curve of her form, every glance from her eyes started to pull him in. Without Tobe realizing it until it was much too late, a door opened into him and she entered. She caught Tobe's "fancy"—with both hands—and would not let go.

The music stopped. The girl with amber hair descended the stairs.

"Can I . . . can I buy you a drink?" Tobe blurted out, surprising himself.

"Sure, sweetie." She grabbed his hand and led him to a table. Tobe noticed how she swung her hips as she walked. They sat down, and a server appeared.

"What can I get you two?" he asked.

"A large bottle of ale, with a shot of vootska on the side." Her voice was strong and confident.

The server nodded and then looked at Tobe. "And for you?"

"Ah . . . an ale should do me fine," Tobe said, stammering a bit.

The girl leaned forward, close to Tobe's face. "Do you think I am pretty?"

Before Tobe could answer, a man came up and plopped down in a chair next to the girl. He placed his hand on her. He was not a stranger. "I will see you later," he said, slurring his words. He rose, swaying back and forth, looking down at the girl.

"Oh, go away. Leave us alone," said the girl to the man. Tobe could see she loved the attention.

Playfully, the man lightly slapped her on the cheek. He looked at Tobe with an out-of-focus gaze. "Be careful of this one! She will eat you alive." He then staggered off.

Tobe was starting to feel strange and self-conscious—small—like a naïve little boy. It was becoming clear she was out of his league—a league he had no desire to play in.

She leaned in closer, as she played with a button on Tobe's shirt. She asked again, with all her seductive charm, "Well, do you find me pretty?"

Tobe looked closely at her. Her eyes did not sparkle. They were dull from dreams and illusions that filled her mind. Beyond that, Tobe perceived in them a shadow world of wounds and dark laments, spiced with a sprinkling of self-loathing and despair, which all her feigned frivolity could not disguise.

Another fellow came up, kissed the girl on the cheek, and took her hand. She looked at him with a flirtatious grin.

"You know I miss you!" he said playfully, with a touch of cynicism. "Remember, you are *mine.*" Then he, too, left.

The drinks came. She threw down the shot of Vootska and chased it with the ale. Tobe's impression of the girl kept changing. He could see that, in the beginning, he had woven a picture of her in his mind out of pure imagination. He was never attracted to *her* at all, but to his *idea* of her. He was astounded at how easily he could be swept up by nothing more than an *illusion* of someone!

The girl finished off the bottle. "I have to go. Don't go away." She kissed Tobe hard on the lips, in a calloused, self-absorbed way. She rushed to the stage as the music began, kicking her legs in the air once again.

Tobe's insides started to twist in knots. He spiraled down to a raw and painful place, and from there looked out upon his world. It was a different world—and it was not a happy one. He murmured aloud, "Dancing bones, eyeballs turning in boned sockets, all decorated with a sugar frosting made of perfumed skin." The whole while, he was seeing the emptiness and suffering on the dancing girls' faces. *What's really going on here?*

"'Dancing bones, eyeballs in boned sockets'? Getting a little glum, are we?"

Tobe turned. It was Sebastian. He looked bright and cheery—a breath of fresh air.

"Glum?" replied Tobe, "Too serious? Perhaps."

Yet Tobe could feel his mood brighten. He was relieved to smile at his friend. "But Sebastian, it's true. Just look!"

Sebastian sat down next to Tobe. He briefly glanced at the girls and then turned back toward Tobe. "You should have come with us," said Sebastian. "We did some great things. We really changed things up." (Tobe had his doubts.)

Sebastian turned his gaze back to the dancing girls, and this time he could not turn away. "Wow, look where you ended up! Man, they sure are pretty!" Sebastian, too, was hooked.

Tobe couldn't take it anymore. He got up from the table. "I have to go. Are you ready?"

"What? I just got here! Your eyes may be full from devouring these goodies, but I am starving, my friend. You go ahead. I'll catch up."

"Some 'philosopher' you are," Tobe blurted out, surprised by his sudden impatience with his friend.

Sebastian's jaw clenched; he bristled a bit. "And some 'poet' you are!" Tobe could hear the tension mounting in Sebastian's words. "What kind of a poet can you be that doesn't know how to grab life by the hands and enjoy it?"

They stared at each other. Then, Sebastian's expression began to soften. The corners of his mouth took on a hint of a smile. His icy stare began to melt. He chuckled. Tobe could not resist, and they both laughed aloud.

Tobe glanced again at the girls on the stage. Their beauty now appeared pitiful to him, full of seriousness and self-importance. "Look how they are enamored with their own beauty. Even *they* are held in its trance."

"Yes, but they sure *are* beautiful!" said Sebastian.

Tobe turned and started walking away. "Go ahead, 'dine,' my friend. Enjoy yourself. Poet or not, I have to get out of here."

As Tobe walked, words started coming into his head. He took out a pencil and paper and jotted them down:

> The exquisite beauty
> > of the female form;
> > what an irresistible attraction!
> > > They, too, are held in that snare—
> > > chains stronger than iron.
> > (Yet how quickly that beauty fades—
> just a couple decades will do!)

Tobe paused as the perceptions in his mind started shifting; then he went on.

> Yet, I reckon
> > it's not about her. . .nor me, after all.
> > > No, it's about the eggs between those legs,
> > > > that's the purpose of it all!
>
> > > That one day they may hatch
> > and scream out "Ma!" "Pa!"
> that's the purpose of it all!
>
> And you and I, my dear friend,
> > driven insane by our wildly swinging passions,
> > are but pawns in that larger game
> > > . . . after all!

Tobe paused again, and then in big letters he scribbled at the top of the poem:

Scrambled Leggs

"There, that's it." He looked at the poem. He could hear the others say, "Not enough rhyme!" "The meter is all wrong!" "It's nonsense!" He debated whether to throw it away and then folded it up and put it in his pocket.

As Tobe walked through the carnival, it became clear to him that the carnival was not without its perils. Though some aisles had nothing of real value to offer, people still would gladly pay and rush in, blind to any consequence, losing themselves there indefinitely.

Tobe came to a very large tent. The lines were long. Tobe got close enough to read the sign, "The Great War Tent." He was excited. Tales of war, courage, and conquest had always fascinated him.

For sale were "observer" as well as "contestant" tickets. Tobe gladly paid the admission for an observer seat and went in. He was given leaflets with editorials on the conflicting views that would be fought over that day. These differences were to be settled through force and might (as if the power of minds would not do).

Tobe took his seat.

The contestants were mere boys or young men mostly, laughing and joking with each other. Many were captivated by the romantic warrior dream of 'honor,' 'duty,' and the vision of the 'hero.' How they seemed to love the excitement, as they waited for the game to begin.

The young men were then divided into two teams and went off in separate directions. Once they were all suited and buckled up, they shouldered their weapons and re-entered the large tent, one team at either end. Covering the ground was a pattern—exactly like the board on which the power brokers at the high-finance tables played.

The two teams stood there looking at each other. Tobe could feel the tension building. There was a yell. Something was thrown. Someone was hurt. There arose a clamor for retaliation. That was all that was needed. They were ready to attack and kill each other. War was now justified!

A signal sounded. The two teams charged each other, brandishing and swinging their weapons. The sounds were deafening—screams, cries, and shouting along with metal clanging, gun shots, and explosions. Once the fighting started, its momentum quickly escalated out of control.

The field of battle was the scene of a most desperate life-and-death struggle. The smell of fear was heavy in the air. It was not long before blood covered the ground of the arena, with parts of bodies scattered everywhere. The dead and dying were sprawled about, moaning and calling out. Tobe could hardly believe what he was watching. It was no "game"; it had become horribly real. This was so different from how he imagined war in the tales he loved so.

After an hour or so, the conflict was finally resolved—through blood or compromise—and a ceasefire was called. During this pause, both sides started carrying the bodies of their fallen comrades away. Soon new scenarios were announced, replacements brought in, and new teams formed with new alliances. It was not long before the fighting began all over again.

Tobe could not watch any more. He had seen enough. As he walked out, a wounded soldier still on the ground reached up and grabbed his leg. The lower part of the man's face was blown away, leaving a gaping hole.

He desperately wanted to tell Tobe something, but only the wispy sound of air could be heard coming from his open throat. The man's eyes, full of shock, pleaded for something. Whatever it was, Tobe knew, he did not have it to give.

Tobe broke away and did not look back. Of all the tents, The Great War Tent was the saddest and yet, strangely, the most touching. Here and there, Tobe saw such selfless and courageous acts, unequaled by anything he had ever seen anywhere. This was a place where a person would even lay down his life for another. Tobe could not help but feel great admiration for some of those who fought upon this field of madness.

Empathy, too, filled Tobe. The warrior role could turn so tragic. His heart ached for their suffering and for the real price they paid for admittance onto this field of pain. And beneath all the reasons why (and there were always reasons), Tobe wondered, *But why?*

Outside, under the starry night sky, Tobe was not sure how much more of the carnival he could endure. His enthusiasm was dwindling rapidly. He shuffled mechanically down the aisle. The carnival was becoming stranger and stranger.

Clowns passed with grotesque plastic faces. Where before Tobe saw people enjoying the carnival, now everyone seemed frantic. They were stuffing themselves to excess with all that they could eat, taste, and touch—wanting more and more. Beneath it all, he sensed an unacknowledged emptiness and gnawing fear, which all their indulgences could only temporarily conceal.

Though everything is for sale here, nothing here brings lasting joy. I feel no peace in this place. Nothing is more unstable or unpredictable in the whole universe than the minds and hearts of those who journey through this peculiar carnival.

Tobe now saw suffering all about him, disguised in infinite ways. It seemed rare to him that affection flowered long in any heart.

The carnival no longer seemed a place of happy make-believe, but a painful self-centered world—where servants tremble before the king and gladness crumbles away from everything.

Tobe strolled on. He soon came to a large iron gate. Above were the words, "The Carnival Exit." It was draped in black fabric with large black ribbon wreaths. There were caskets lined in rows. Musicians played melancholy melodies, their notes bowing reverently before somber death. Sobbing filled the air. It seemed that death was the only way to leave this carnival.

Carnival II — Tobe's Nightmare

Tobe sensed a horrible spell over the carnival. His world was growing so heavy that he felt that at any moment the stars could lose their grip on the heavens and come tumbling down.

Yes, he knew he had fallen into another dark hole. But he no longer had the strength or will to get out. He let go and fell and fell. As he looked about, the *whole carnival* seemed to be in a dark hole. An icy chill ran up his spine.

An impulse to write pierced his darkness. He welcomed any kind of distraction. He got out a paper and pencil, not knowing what he was going to write.

O Melon Collie

What a strange creature you are.
  Such bitter-tasting fruit,
    spoiled, overripe;
      cloaked in the color dreary—
        world-weary.

O, Melon Collie, what an odd creature you are.
  A one-eyed, mangy dog,
    howling at the wind.
      No answers you have—
        nor hope within.

(I suspect,
  a mere phantom
  of my own weaving.)

Tobe chuckled to himself as he finished this most curious poem. It had done its work; he felt the faintest glow in his heart—giving the poem any real value it might have. *No need to save it for Sebastian. Surely it is "lacking."* He carefully folded it up and threw it away.

He turned away from the exit and continued, slowly sauntering down the isle of tents. He came to a sign that read: "The Great Hall of Mirrors." *Some simple amusement. It will do me well.* Tobe paid the price.

Inside, an upward-slanting ramp led to a door. He entered and was relieved to find himself alone in a long hall, painted in black, lined with mirrors. These were no ordinary mirrors. The first mirror showed him all wavy and distorted. He could hardly recognize himself. Each mirror portrayed him differently, with its own unique exaggerations. He appeared weak, then arrogant, now vulnerable, then thoughtful, now self-centered, then angry, next vengeful, then frightened. Others showed him lost in sadness or comically oblivious. The good as well as the bad oscillated as the mirrors went on and on.

Seeing all these aspects of himself so clearly, in such a short period, had an odd effect. Instead of making it clearer who he was, he started to feel as though he did not know. He felt like a puzzle with the pieces scattered all about. Moreover, the "self" that was supposed to hold all the pieces together seemed to lack any real substance at all.

The last mirror was called "Time." At first when Tobe looked in it, he saw nothing unusual, just the way he normally appeared to himself. Then his image started to melt and change. Smaller and smaller Tobe became, until he was an infant lying in a crib. He had little, pudgy hands, with delicate fingers and the tiniest fingernails. Light shined in those eyes. *Was I that pure and innocent once?*

The image re-formed into a boy playing with stuffed animals and toy soldiers on the bedroom floor; and then, into a youth running in a green field, playing ball with friends. Next, he saw himself with his childhood sweetheart, his heart in its first, intoxicating bloom; and then, later, in his boat on the lake, drawing pictures.

Finally, the image changed to the future: an old man, his body frail and weathered from a life of work. His hands were gnarly and knotted, with clearly delineated bones and serpentine veins. The down-set corners of his mouth and the eyes with no sparkle spoke of loss and regrets—of an unfulfilled life. Death was approaching. He was taking his last slow breaths.

So this is how it ends; this is what I come to. Tobe was stunned. He felt a sting of pain. *I squandered my life. . . . No, it does not have end like this! I will not let it end like this!*

All the lights went out in The Hall of Mirrors. Everything became pitch black. He could see at the end of the hall a faint crack of light around a door. He made his way toward it, pushed it open, and stepped out into the carnival night. The air was cool.

Tobe thought about who he was and about his life. He was confused—confused by it all. He had no answers. *My life is a tale written in some code I don't understand. What it all means, I have no idea. I feel like a dream of somebody—and not the real thing at all.* Tobe looked up. A vast, starry sky flowed into him, soothing his aching soul.

"Are you OK?" Again, Sebastian's voice pierced Tobe's world.

Tobe turned. "It sure is great to see you. What a nightmare!"

They stood together, silently. Tobe sighed. "Sebastian, I don't want or need anything from this place!"

It was then, in that split second as he uttered those words, that Tobe finally remembered. For the first time in a very long time, Tobe remembered the word, *Inlăkesh*.

"I think I know what you need," said Sebastian. "It's over here."

They walked down a side aisle until they came to a tent with a simple hand-carved sign: "Books." Tobe was drawn instantly to the place. As he walked, he looked back at Sebastian.

"Aren't you coming?"

"No, go ahead. I have something to do. I'm going to the War Tent— some things in this world you just have to fight for." Sebastian turned and started walking away.

Tobe desperately wanted to warn him. "Wait! Why, Sebastian? Don't do it!"

Sebastian kept walking and then turned. Smiling, he said, "Take care, Tobe. Don't worry; I will be fine."

Tobe knew he could say nothing to change Sebastian's mind.

Tobe stood there, unable to shake the feeling that it would be the last time he would ever see Sebastian. Sadly, he turned. He removed his hat, letting it fall from his hands into a barrel. He grabbed the flap covering the entrance to the book tent, drew it aside, and stepped in.

CHAPTER FIVE

The Bookseller

*The bridge between that world and this is so little and so easy
to cross, that you could not believe it is the meeting place of
worlds so different. Yet this little bridge is the strongest thing
that touches on this world at all.*

A Course in Miracles

 NSIDE THE TENT WAS a different world, filled with books—books on shelves and in stacks piled high on colorful, ornate carpets. Plants in pots, small paintings, and little statues were scattered about, creating a most pleasant effect. Everything was bathed in a soft light and a welcoming hush. It was a soothing place, healing every sore and wound Tobe carried.

Sitting at a desk was an older man with clear eyes behind gold-rimmed spectacles, boney features, and gray hair pulled back neatly in a tail. He observed Tobe briefly and then returned to his writing, saying "Please, take a look around . . . take your time. 'Tobe'—am I correct?"

"Yes, that's my name, but how did you . . ."

The man's eyes fleetingly met Tobe's. "It's a long story that dances on a pin . . . written long ago. Things are connected in ways you don't understand, with layers to everything," he said, finishing his sentence with a smile and a sparkle in his eye.

Tobe smiled back. He liked this fellow.

Tobe looked around the tent. The paintings were mostly landscapes and portraits of poets and saints. A peculiar one, painted in a free-spirited hand, caught his attention. He was not sure what the image was. It looked like a knocked-over vase . . . or perhaps a fish. It had an orange glow and streaks of blue—almost like lightning along its sides. One thing was sure: it had been painted by an untrained hand.

"It's one I did," said bookseller. "The technique could be better. But look at that eye; it can see *everything*! Some things are so incredible; you just have to paint them."

Tobe, being polite, said, "It's nice." However, he was still not sure what it was, and he did not dare ask, lest he hurt the bookseller's feelings. Another picture attracted Tobe's eye. He welcomed the chance to speak about something different.

"This one is interesting," Tobe said.

"Ah, that is one of my favorites," said the bookseller. "It is from a time long gone by—a saint with his mischievous little demons. Look at the saint's smile, and the focus and peace in his eyes—while all that nonsense is going on. He is grounded in his God and sees only Him. *Nothing* distracts him; his bliss cannot be shaken. Now, that is how one should live in this world!"

The bookseller looked at Tobe and asked, "And how can I help you today?"

Tobe paused to think. "I was reading a book about a place called 'Inlăkesh' and the 'River Is' . . ."

"I know that book well. It is a good one. That is why I was told to send it to you. And look, it did its work; it brought you here."

What the bookseller said got Tobe's mind spinning, filled with questions; when it finally cleared a bit, he went back to what he was going to ask at first, saving all his other questions for later. "Do you have any books that tell how I might get to Inlăkesh . . . or any maps?"

The bookseller rose and went over to a shelf. "I have both books and maps in abundance. For example, here is a map. . . ." He patted a large, folded-up bundle that filled the whole shelf. "If I opened it up and unrolled it, it would fill this whole tent."

"It's huge! What a long journey that must be." Tobe remarked.

"I have smaller maps," said the bookseller, "where the journey takes much less time. They are better. And better yet are the tiny maps you can put on the tip of your finger! Those journeys take no time at all. Yet the curious thing about Inlăkesh that I have experienced—"

Saint Tempted by Demons

"You have been to Inlākesh?!" Tobe's face lit up.

"Oh yes," the bookseller said.

"You have seen the River Is?!"

"Yes, I swim in It every chance I get."

Tobe stood there, dumbfounded.

"You can get to Inlākesh in many ways," continued the bookseller. "You don't need legs to get there, though some prefer to think they do. Only the thinnest of veils separates you from it—a veil as insubstantial as a whisper."

The bookseller rearranged some books as he spoke. "It's better to think of Inlākesh not as a place, but as a *dimension*. It vibrates at a quicker frequency and permeates this dense world we are in—the way light can shine through stained glass. Or, one could say, Inlākesh intersects this world like the warp, the vertical fibers in a weaving, through which are woven the colored threads that make up the images of this world. So you can see that big maps are quite unnecessary, and getting there need not take any time at all."

Though Tobe couldn't quite wrap his mind around what the bookseller was saying, he could feel his enthusiasm rising.

"Portals are even here in the carnival." The bookseller paused, "Are you interested?"

Tobe blurted out, "Where?"

"Have a seat." The bookseller motioned to a chair near his desk. "I want to tell you a few things first. The first thing: To find a portal one must believe Inlākesh *really* does exist. This takes faith . . . until one *actually* goes there.

"Secondly, a person must *truly* desire to go there. Desire attracts the portal like a magnet. Yet as much as one may think one wants Inlākesh with all one's heart, responsibilities, delays, and deviations come up—and down cul-de-sacs we go. We create all of it to get lost in the world again. We lose ourselves and fool ourselves endlessly. Some tea?"

"Yes, please."

The bookseller rose and went to a little stove. There was the sound of the tinkling of china and silver, and soon he was back with two cups on a tray.

"Here you are," the bookseller said, as he placed the tray on a stand next to Tobe. He continued, "It is important to see that, in spite of all our longing, a part of us doesn't *really* want to go there. That part is afraid of it. That's why all the big maps, of which I sell quite a few."

As Tobe took a sip of tea, he thought of how incredibly fortunate he was to have found someone who actually knew about Inlākesh and had been there!

As if the bookseller were reading Tobe's thoughts, he asked, "Would you like to go there *now*?"

The words took Tobe by surprise. He felt nervous, yet excited.

"Yes, I would," Tobe said, flustered.

"Come, I will take you to my favorite place. I sit there for hours at a time looking at the carnival. It is amazing where you can go just sitting in one place!"

Tobe grabbed his backpack and followed the bookseller out of the tent and through the crowd. They cut into the shadows and made their way to a well-disguised hole in the fence that surrounded the carnival.

They slipped through the opening and across a flat plain that led to the base of a ridge and began their climb. At the top was a rock outcropping. They went out to the very edge and sat down. The climb and fresh air energized Tobe. In the distance, under the night sky, was the carnival. It was a relief to be away from its craziness.

The bookseller, looking over the carnival with a calm gaze, said, "Have you ever seen anything more incredible? Something wonderful is in each living soul walking about down there. They are truly extraordinary—so beautiful, but like you, they don't know it."

Tobe was taken aback. He wondered what the bookseller saw. It was definitely a different world from what he saw.

"I don't know," said Tobe, trying to be as honest as he could. "In the beginning, I did enjoy the carnival; I was happy there. But after awhile, things began to change. Everything started to feel futile and valueless. It turned into a place of pain and madness." Tobe picked up a pebble and tossed it inattentively over the edge. "How can you see something 'wonderful' in each person down there? They seem empty—and completely lost in themselves and in their world."

"Do not be too hasty to judge," said the bookseller. "Yes, it is true: the carnival can appear to be a place of pain and suffering. Yet a light shines in the carnival, as well as in each and every person down there. It shines through everything with great power. Nothing is dense enough to hold back this light."

It sounds too fantastic.

"I see you don't quite believe it," said the bookseller. "But you will. You will see it with your own eyes. It is OK that you find the people and the carnival lacking. If you had not been disappointed, you would not be here now; you would still be down there, lost in some shallow amusement. Your life is about something different now, something bigger." The bookseller paused. "Are you ready to go to Inlăkesh?"

"Yes, I am," Tobe said without hesitating. He was relieved to find that all his nervousness was gone.

"To have the portal open up to you," continued the bookseller, "you will first need to get rid of what stands in the way of your seeing it—all that unnecessary inner clutter—all those heavy thoughts and feelings. You will be vibrating too low to see it, even though it is right in front of you."

Tobe was ready to let go of everything that stood in the way, and he could already see some of the blocks in himself: all those heavy, dense emotions. He did not wait. He remembered an old fairy tale of a Prince who used a sacred fire to free his kingdom from a darkness. *Why not try it now?* Tobe imagined flames inside himself. He could feel them growing. These were not angry flames; a benevolence was in them. He watched them consume every thought and every feeling.

He also gathered up every weakness and fear he could observe in himself, as well as the ones he could not see but knew were there. He fed them all to the cleansing flames. When he forgot and the fire went out, he lit the inner flames again. He gave it *all* up to the flames—even everything he called "Tobe." He waited to see what remained. It was soothing to let go of *everything.* "House on Fire," he called it, and from that day on, it never left him for long.

When Tobe felt the burning was complete and all the flames had died down, 'he' was still there, but now he felt quiet and empty inside, and full of clarity.

"Very good," said the bookseller, studying Tobe closely. "And you did that all by yourself. *Now* you will be able to see the portal."

The bookseller paused to take in the night, and then said, "The quicker vibration of Inlăkesh, as I said earlier, makes Inlăkesh shine through the things of this dense world. You can see it shining through in the beauty of things: in their perfection and in their life. If you are still and go deep into all these things, you will see the portal start opening up to you. To start, just tell yourself everything is perfect, whole, and glorious—with no spot of darkness anywhere in it—no matter what you are looking on. Though your eyes do not see it, do not question or hesitate. Then surrender and watch the perceptions of your world begin to shift before you as the portal to Inlăkesh opens up. Are you ready?"

Tobe had never felt more ready for anything, but he could not help but feel that surely there must be more. Tobe doubted something so simple could really be a portal to a whole new world. "That's all?" Tobe asked.

"Yes. It sounds simple and it *is*, as most important things are. This is the tiniest map I have. It's the quickest and easiest way . . . if you are ready for it."

"When the portal comes," continued the bookseller, "remember, just let go. The love of Inläkesh will draw you up to itself. You will know when you are approaching Inläkesh, for you will feel a deep peace, and time will seem to stand still."

The bookseller grew quiet. Tobe looked at the landscape before him, and the carnival below filled with people. He tried to see them all as "perfect, whole, and glorious—with no spot of darkness anywhere."

After a few moments he said, "Nothing is happening. I see everything the same."

"Be still," said the bookseller. "Do not doubt, and try again. And then again. You have all the time in the world."

The bookseller rose and, touching Tobe on the shoulder, said, "I have done all I can. The rest is up to you. This is *your* time. This is what you came here for." He then headed off into the night, leaving Tobe sitting alone, overlooking the carnival.

Tobe desperately wanted the bookseller to stay. *No, Don't go! Not now! This is when I need you most!* He could hear his voice yelling inside his head. Then just as he was about to speak, a powerful calm came over him. He took in a few deep breaths, letting the fresh air from the night flow into him. He began to feel lighter. He settled into the night. He relaxed, and time passed. Slowly things began to shift as he looked on everything as "perfect, whole, and glorious—with no spot of darkness anywhere in it."

The carnival started to appear enchanting. Its lights sparkled with welcome; tiny specks of people moved about with unhurried tranquility. A delightful charm radiated from the carnival. The starry night above held the world in its gentle hands; its peace flowed into Tobe. Everything glowed with perfection, bathed in a loveliness, profound and deep. Each moment grew richer, with one wonder after another revealing itself to him. Time stood still.

Tobe did not realize it, but he *was* in the portal! And he was rising! Rising through it, drawn by the love of Inläkesh *drawing Tobe to itself*!

CHAPTER SIX

"Welcome to Inlăkesh"

Wonder is the beginning of wisdom.

Socrates

LOATING THROUGH LAYERS OF light, Tobe continued to ascend. Gradually the movement began to slow, and then it ceased altogether. Tobe could feel his feet gently coming to rest on something solid. In an instant, his mind cleared and he felt oriented again. He opened his eyes and looked around. A light with a new kind of brilliance filled the air and bathed everything. His eyes slowly adjusted.

He discovered he was standing at the edge of a small lake. Green hills, dotted with a few well-cared-for homes, gave way in the distance to a rich, deep evergreen sea of trees. The forest extended up to the base of pointy-peaked mountains capped with snow—all clearly reflected in the lake.

The air was thin and clean, with fragrances rising from the rich earth and all the growing things. The restful silence, punctuated by the occasional call of birds, joined the peaceful rhythm of the lake's liquid lapping at the shore. Above, glowing white clouds moved in a deep hush.

Like elegant dancers gliding across the blue dance floor of the sky, Tobe mused.

The sky was a rich, pure blue, the purest blue Tobe had ever seen. It turned an even richer and deeper shade of blue the higher he looked.

Then a slight breeze blew over the surface of the lake, breaking up the reflected images into little waves, with dancing sparkles of sunlight. When the breeze passed, all settled back into stillness again, and the clear reflection returned.

In the green fringe of reeds and willows near the shore, a noble, solitary heron stood vigil. Then a pair of white swans came visiting, flying in with wings outstretched. Smooth and slow, they descended to the water. With a final flapping of their wings, they both rose, almost vertically, and then, with the slightest splash, landed and settled into a smooth glide. Their image was mirrored on the glassy surface of the lake. *How like an apparition—like two angelic spirits, they float.*

Tobe looked down. The leaf of a plant called to him in its flawlessness. He took a moment to kneel and admire it. Its delicate thinness and intricate design, the tiny veins running throughout; the entire leaf was so filled with life. It was a miracle to behold!

Sky, mountains, trees, and lake were all playing their song in perfect harmony. This world, overflowing with life—lush and green, ripe and delicious upon itself, made Tobe feel he was awake in a beautiful dream.

"Welcome to Inlãkesh."

The voice startled Tobe. It took him a fraction of second to realize it was the Bookseller. Tobe turned and was surprised by his appearance. He had changed somehow. His eyes were brighter. A radiance seemed to emanate from him.

"You seem a bit bewildered, Tobe."

"It's just that you appear . . . different."

"I've always been this way," said the Bookseller. "It is *you* who are different. You are now seeing with the eyes of Inlãkesh." The Bookseller seemed ecstatic as he perused the landscape. "Now you *know* Inlãkesh is not just the stuff of books and tales. It's quite wonderful isn't it?"

Tobe followed the Bookseller's gaze. Everything resembled the things of Soñadora in every way, except that here, colors seemed brighter, fragrances sweeter, and sounds clearer. Everything sparkled and sang with a purity. Something in the air told Tobe that this place was full of secrets that would gladly reveal themselves—if he were still enough, and *brave* enough.

"Yes, it is . . . unbelievable." Tobe could not shake the feeling he was *awake* in a dream. "And the portal worked, just as you said."

"It's the miracle of Inlãkesh," the Bookseller replied. "Your heart called to it, and it pulled you through the portal to itself!"

Tobe relished every impression as each freely entered and energized him. "In the old world, forms seem so utterly dense . . .," Tobe said. "Dull in comparison—covered in heavy opaque wrappings, where no light of life can get out, and keeping its life like a secret within." (Tobe was surprised he could express it so clearly. He was just beginning to find out that putting meaning to words came much easier in Inlăkesh.) "But here . . .," Tobe paused to give his mind time to put it just right. "Here, the life in everything joyously glows beyond its skin!"

The Bookseller smiled. "That, Tobe, is because the River Is flows freely here."

Tobe's hopes rose. "Where?"

"Patience. In due time. I can tell you this. It is invisible, yet, closer than close, flowing underneath everything. Then suddenly you will see It rise to the surface, making Itself known! And you will see It flow so strongly, that It will be seen *everywhere* and all at once!"

All this was too much for Tobe to comprehend.

The Bookseller looked at Tobe and said, "It has been marvelous to see you here in Inlăkesh!" He paused, "Well, I'd best be going. No doubt someone is looking for a book right about now. Don't worry; you'll be fine. Shortly, someone will come to guide you through this world. Take care, Tobe."

The Bookseller smiled and walked away. As Tobe watched, a dozen questions came to his mind. "Wait!" he called out, but the Bookseller was already beyond the range of hearing. He turned and waved before disappearing, as he entered a grove of trees.

Finding himself alone in this new land, a feeling of anxiety passed through Tobe's body. *An old habit.* Yet, as quickly as those feelings arose, a gentle force washed them away, for no darkness is strong enough or real enough to exist in Inlăkesh for long.

In the nearby bushes, Tobe heard a rustling noise. It grew louder. A vague shimmering outline started to appear—partially visible and gradually more distinct. Finally, stepping out from the bushes, emerged a child. Although the child wore boy's clothes, Tobe was not sure whether it was a boy or girl, for its features were fair. He looked closer. The child appeared no more than twelve years of age. The hair was wild and unruly. The clothes were dirty and torn, here and there. The child was slightly out of breath, as if coming from playing some rough-and-tumble outdoor sport.

The child said nothing, looking at Tobe with a curious little smile. Its piercing yet playful eyes had a mischievous, untamed quality in them.

What troublesome creature is this? Tobe mused.

Then the child spoke, "You must be 'Tobe.'"

"I am." Tobe said, surprised the child knew.

"I will be your *guide*," the child said in a proud tone.

Tobe felt a sharp stab of disappointment. *This mere infant is not fit to be anybody's guide.*

With arms extended wide, as if to gather in the whole world, the child suddenly spun around, and with face beaming in enthusiasm, said, "Mr. Tobe, welcome to Inlākesh . . . and the wonder of your mind!"

Tobe stood there silently observing the peculiar scene. The child's words echoed in his head. *"The wonder of your mind"—whatever does that mean?* It made no sense to Tobe. Furthermore, his mind felt anything but "wondrous."

"Oh, I'm sorry," said the child, as if noticing Tobe's consternation. "I am getting a little ahead of myself. Forget that I said that last bit. It's way too soon for that."

"No harm done, I'm sure," said Tobe, dropping the whole thing. *What a curious creature!*

"Inlākesh is a most extraordinary place!" said the child. "Unlike other worlds, what you call miracles are the most common thing here!" The child, with boundless energy, was in constant movement: sitting, standing, and rocking back and forth. The child continued, "Miracles are everywhere, and each moment overflows with them!"

Tobe was befuddled by the contradiction—though the child's voice was youthful and actions adolescent, for sure, there was a curious maturity in the child's choice of words.

"Are you a boy or a girl—if you don't mind my asking?"

"My name is Auriel," she said as she curtsied. She paused for a moment, looking closely at Tobe. "I'm sorry to disappoint you. I can see that I am not what you had in mind for a guide. I will try to be more serious and do my best to act . . . my 'age.'"

That did not console Tobe in the least.

Auriel stood straight, wiped off her clothes, tucked in her shirt, and tried her best to put her hair in some semblance of order. "There, how's that?"

Tobe did not notice much difference, but he did appreciate her attempts to please. And he did notice that there was a charm about her. Her playfulness was starting to delight him—somewhat. His reservations toward her started slipping away, ever so slightly.

"What is it you wish this fine day from Inlăkesh, Tobe?" Auriel asked with a spunky grin.

He thought about her question and did not have to think long. He had but one desire: to find the River of which the poet spoke so lovingly—the River that was in his dream. He spoke with confidence. "I would like to see the *River Is*."

"Better than that, not only will we have you 'seeing' It. We'll have you *swimming* in It! Now, it really doesn't matter in which direction we go; we will surely run into It."

Tobe observed Auriel looking at him with the most curious little smile. Her smile, as if by magic, started turning his inner world aglow.

"Though the River flows everywhere," Auriel continued, "where It can be seen changes from moment to moment." She now looked at Tobe with an air of seriousness. "It can be far away or very close, *depending on you*. It is *our* sight that fluctuates. The River is *constant*!"

Again, Tobe was not sure he understood, but he did not have to think about it. Auriel started walking, gesturing for Tobe to follow.

"Come, let's go on a *real* journey!" she said. Tobe quickly caught up.

"I would like to show you many things," Auriel said. "And don't worry, the River *will* come . . . when the time is right. It delights in your knowing It. And the day you swim in It, It will overflow with joy!"

They were on a path wide enough for two. They strolled casually, speaking of the weather and simple things, as people do when they are first getting to know each other. Tobe spoke to her as someone older speaking to a child. Auriel played along. When asked about herself, she gave thoughtful yet brief replies. Mostly she spoke about things at hand or asked about him.

The path led them around the lake to the far side. Auriel and Tobe crossed a stream on a little wooden bridge. The stream flowed away from the lake, with the path running parallel. As they followed it, Auriel's face took on a playful expression as she looked at the stream and said, "This is *not* the River Is." A few steps further she added, "Though the River Is contains rivers and streams, It is not made of water at all—not *one* drop! It is made of something very different."

Tobe realized he did not have the slightest clue about the River Is.

The clear, cool water of the stream sparkled with light, and ripples crested into little whitecaps. It flowed on, singing its soothing gurgling song. It sang in harmony with the clear calls of birds, creating delightful layers of sound. Moss on rocks and plants on the shore turned brilliant glowing green where lit by the sun. Tobe noticed how the water seemed to *lovingly* caress the rocks in the stream. *No stream in Soñadora does this.* He then sensed the breadth of time, and how whole ages had come and gone as those rocks sat there, in deep contentment. *No rocks in Soñadora sit in deep contentment! And they are not alive like this! What kind of fantastic place is this?*

Then Tobe began to notice something peculiar. The rocks seemed to hum—with *life*. He had a strong sense that the rocks were emitting tones, and every part of each and every rock seemed to be playing a different tone. Though his ear could not hear the tones, he *could* perceive them. He thought, *If I were a musician, I would play the rocks! Or I could paint the different tones in bright colors—not how the rocks look at all, but how they feel to the eye! What a strange painting that would be!*

Then it dawned on Tobe: *in Inlăkesh the eye can actually* feel! *How bizarre!*

He was elated to find that not only did each part of a rock have a voice and sing, but every reed and willow, every ripple and wave, and every part of a blade of grass on the bank did. Every inch of everything everywhere was playing a note! Yes, Inlăkesh was *alive!*

"There is truly so much to see here . . . so much to feel here," said Tobe. He grew silent in his amazement, absorbing the world about him.

The path veered away from the stream into a rich, green meadow like a carpet stretched on rolling hills, where sheep contentedly grazed. In the folds of the hills, clouds of mist rose with the warmth of the sun, swirling, glowing white—the earth's gift of moisture given back to the sky from the night's rain. Trees gathered in clans in the ravines and in thick groves on the edges of the meadow, their leaves shimmering in the light, and the needles of evergreens glistening with dew. Here and there, a farm could be seen, nestled among trees.

Everything was bathed in a peace so thick upon the place that Tobe felt he could easily grab it out of the air and hold it in his hands. He marveled as he realized *peace existed in the air! Yes, space, too, was alive in Inlăkesh!* Before now, Tobe had thought that the only things living in space were the things which moved through it, like dragonflies, butterflies, and such things.

The path went up a hill and into a grove of trees, running along the crest. Tobe and Auriel entered the grove. A breeze sent the leaves clapping in soft applause, as if in welcome, and the evergreens hummed softly with their deep-toned "Om-m-m." White tree trunks glowed brilliantly where touched by the sun. Tobe was sure he could sense the trees communicating to each other and to him, in some unknown tongue, though he did not have the ears to quite perceive it.

He noticed that his awareness was sharper in Inlākesh, giving rise to peculiar perceptions. Things that in the past he did not see or took for granted now seemed grand and mysterious. Tobe saw his hands as strange, alien things, as if from another world. When he looked closely at the hairs on his arms and the back of his hands, he was shocked. Growing from porous skin, they seemed more fitting of some kind of beast than what he imagined he was!

And he felt his legs and feet trudging up and down the uneven ground— hard workers—while his head and torso smoothly glided above, without a care, occupied only with emotions and perceptions. *How strange. They are like two different worlds, under different laws, yet how beautifully they work together.*

As Tobe observed that thought and it faded away, he wondered, *How is it possible that I even have something as rarified as a thought—as fine as air, floating in this hard-boned, domed skull? Where, in all the universe, is there such a strange phenomenon? Or is it an illusion, and thoughts are everywhere and freer than I think—and no skull can hold them at all?*

Auriel was silently watching Tobe. She said, "Try looking out of your face. It is the most curious thing."

Tobe wasn't sure what she meant at first, but then suddenly, his head felt like a giant eye of pure seeing, looking out and absorbing everything. The "seeing" was so strong that the sensation of his physical face faded away completely, as if he didn't have a face at all!

As they continued to walk, Tobe's attention returned to the landscape. He was drawn to the colorful rocks, sprinkled about the grove like jewels, and to the flowers in bright colors of yellow, violet, and blue. Small mushrooms on thin stems grew under ferns; and heartier mushrooms, red ones with white spots, grew among the grass in the full sun. Around every turn of the path, breathtaking views of rolling hills and tall mountains opened up.

Tobe asked Auriel, "What are they like . . . the people that live here?

"They are beautiful," said Auriel. "They are a delight to be around. They are friendly and cheerful. They love to laugh and are quick to join in a conversation. They are patient. They are glad to let go of any angst or upset, even before they can hold it. They have no bad will toward anything." Auriel paused. "Above all, they want what you want—to swim in the River Is."

Hearing Auriel speak gave Tobe pause. She was intelligent and full of insight, way beyond her years. He realized how unfair his judgments of her had been.

As if Auriel could read his mind, she said, "It doesn't matter how you felt about me. It did not touch me." She took Tobe's hand like a caring mother and, looking him in the eyes, said, "Judgments are riddled with errors. See how yours are already shifting and passing away. We see things with only what little understanding we have. Inlăkesh has much to teach you. One day you will see things very differently. Then you will be done with judging. Can you imagine how marvelous things will appear then, and how great you will feel?"

Tobe realized he had never been more wrong about anyone. He now saw Auriel in a totally different light. Her child frame, her disheveled appearance belied her wisdom. She was something he could not even begin to fathom. What he had thought was wildness in her eyes, he now knew was the light of pure, unbridled being and innocence. What had made him feel uneasy when he first looked into her eyes was her freedom and power—*because I am afraid of my own.*

Auriel, pulling Tobe by the hand, started walking quickly and then gaily trotted as she laughed. "Isn't it wonderful to be alive in Inlăkesh!"

When they finally slowed to a walk, Tobe asked, "Can you read minds?"

Tobe did not hear her answer, for just then, a leaf blew across the path, shooting off little sparks of mathematical equations as it went! Remarkably, the equations were defining its every move as it tumbled and spun. Then, in a gap in the tree canopy above, Tobe could see birds flying. Every flap of their wings, their every twist and turn, their soaring and diving, their coming together and going apart—*all* became mathematical equations.

As Tobe looked about, he saw that the shape and design of everything had a mathematical perfection: in the plants and the trees, even down to the tiny crystals on the rocks. All was pure mathematics, living geometry! Tobe wondered what force could bring such exquisite order into dense matter. Even in the distant mountains and in the clouds above—in the light and in the interaction and harmony of all things, he sensed equations. Space itself was *alive* with the dance of them. Formulas were everywhere, spinning life into manifestation and holding everything into being. Living numbers filled Inlăkesh to the brim!

Auriel and Tobe Walking through the Wonders of Inlākesh

If only I could get at them so I could write them down!

Tobe loved mathematical equations, though he did not know much about them. As early as he could remember, he would sit transfixed as he studied them in books or on blackboards. How eloquently they pointed to the truth in the things of the world, and even beyond. But what a joy it was to see math like this, alive and moving about! This math breathed and had fire in its eyes—a math of real power—with divine magic in it! How all this was possible, Tobe had no idea, but this was Inlăkesh. And here, he was finding, anything was possible!

Though Tobe did not know exactly what the equations were, he knew that they were ripe and ready for someone to come along and pluck them, and to give them to the world.

As Tobe watched, the equations began to fade.

"Those mathematical doorways are a different way of seeing," said Auriel. "Some people stay in that reality for long periods of time; some even *live* there."

Auriel excitedly touched Tobe's arm and continued, "Can you imagine a formula for the River Is? No one has discovered that one yet, but wouldn't that be extraordinary?"

"Yes," said Tobe as he wondered at the spirit of numbers to do such extraordinary things.

"This living mathematics," added Auriel, "is just one of thousands of tales Inlăkesh has to tell you. Miracles are endless in Inlăkesh, and it wants to share them all with you."

CHAPTER SEVEN
Deeper into Inlăkesh

Heaven is under our feet as well as over our heads.
Henry David Thoreau

URIEL AND TOBE FOLLOWED the path as it gently cut down from the crest of the hill to the stream below. The path meandered past towering rocks like noble statues, as if blessing all who passed below. As they traveled, the rocks grew taller and tighter together, forming huge cliffs on either side creating a narrow canyon. Out of the cliffs, the occasional tree stubbornly grew. In the canyon, the trail made its way through smoothed archways in the rocks, carved by the stream over the millennia.

"Do you feel how alive this space is?" Auriel asked, looking around in the canyon. Her expression was one of deep concentration.

Tobe did not respond with words. He paused in silence and "looked" at space. He remembered when he felt peace in the air just a little ways back, when he felt he could grab peace and hold it in his hands. Even as Auriel's words hung in the air, Tobe started to *see* and *sense* the very life of space.

"Remember this. It is a glimpse into a new, vast world," Auriel said.

As they walked, Tobe kept looking at space, trying to feel its life. The more he focused on it, the more alive it became.

The path wound its way on the canyon floor around giant boulders, fallen long ago from the towering cliffs above. The whole canyon, rich in vegetation, appeared like a glorious garden. *The expression of some harmonious celestial impulse!*

There were vines, ripe with grapes and luscious berries, and a variety of fruits from trees—all ready to eat. There were nuts from the cones of certain pines and edible leaves of some plants, all creating a cornucopia of simple eating delights to sustain travelers as they went.

Auriel picked a red berry and held it out. "Here, this one is for you."

Tobe took the wild berry and put it in his mouth. His mouth came alive as the berry released its gift of flavors to dance upon his tongue—a kaleidoscope of layers of taste, blending from sweet to tart. All he could say was, "Um-m-m . . . *Delicious!*"

Sounds of the stream and the songs of birds echoed in the canyon, blending with the occasional rumble of the storm above. Tobe noticed he walked with a lighter step, as if there were less gravity in Inlăkesh. His heart felt lighter too.

Auriel and Tobe started to hear voices in conversation in the distance. A family rounded the curve on the trail ahead—a mother, father, and three young children, dressed in simple clothes, neat in appearance. They were carrying blankets and baskets.

These were the first people of Inlăkesh, besides Auriel, that Tobe had seen. As they drew closer, he noticed his excitement mounting. *Now I get to see what they are like!* The family was now upon them. Auriel and Tobe stepped aside. They all shared friendly glances as they passed.

As Auriel and Tobe started walking again, Tobe said, "They appeared friendly and self-assured, but I wasn't able to see much beyond that— nothing unusual or exceptional. What did I miss?"

"You missed a great deal, but don't be concerned about that," said Auriel. "Soon enough you will see very differently."

Walking on, the walls of the canyon started to spread farther and farther apart, like arms opening wide, opening up into a huge green meadow. The sky was large once again, too, filled with white clouds. Tobe marveled at the sky's vast beauty. *A living cosmos unto itself, with its own unique laws—very different from the world of solid things, where my body moves.*

The clouds appeared like an armada of white ships on a blue sea, sailing with the wind. As they approached the distant mountain peaks, they began to collide and merge into one another, building up and becoming dark and dramatic—turning to shades of beautiful, somber blue and gray, appearing like a stormy sea with waves crashing in slow motion up against the mountain peaks—all upside down as Tobe looked up.

Tobe imagined painting the clouds with creamy luscious paint, thick upon the bristles of a big, round brush. He could feel his hand moving the brush as it went gliding across the canvas, blending the rich blue and purple-gray hues, from darkest darks to warm whites—the dramatic clouds merging and swirling thick upon the canvas! What fun!

Suddenly, with a buzz, an insect flew by Tobe, breaking his playful reverie. In that brief instant, he caught a glimpse of the being-ness in the insect's eyes. It was *humongous* and *glorious* inside, not limited at all by its tiny size! This was very strange, for back in Soñadora an insect was always a little thing.

As Auriel and Tobe continued on the path, a few more insects took to flight. Soon the air was alive with the hum of their minikin wings. Tobe could see in the eyes of each insect a doorway that led into its vast being-ness—a dimension of its own. Space became filled with all these "dimensions" flying about, each infinite and alive, coming together in the space/time dimension where Tobe stood!

As he looked about, he marveled, saying to Auriel, "The depth of Inlăkesh has no end!"

Auriel grinned, "Ah, the *miracles* of Inlăkesh!"

Something caught Tobe's eye. He looked closer. It was a girl standing on a slight rise across the stream. She was wearing a cowboy hat and boots with spurs, and next to her was a horse and a pile of rope. She had tied the rope into a lasso and was twirling it above her head. Round and round it went with ease.

Auriel walked on, leaving Tobe to investigate the cowgirl and to study her technique. The lasso expanded out farther and farther. In awe, Tobe watched as he walked closer.

"This is nothing, my friend," she said as Tobe got near. "A lasso spins inside my heart that holds the whole universe . . . and *beyond*!" She looked at Tobe with a friendly smile. "Do you want to be *vast* like that? You will be. You are going to the *River*."

Tobe paused to contemplate her words. He had no response except to smile. He would have stayed longer, for the cowgirl fascinated him, but he did not want Auriel to get too far ahead, and with a step, he was on his way again.

"Swim deep in the River!" called out the cowgirl.

As Tobe walked, the sound of cascading water got louder and louder. He could see Auriel in the meadow, way off in the distance. When he finally reached her, the scene took his breath away. They were standing on

The Being of Insects and the Cowgirl

the very edge of a precipice, a sheer drop-off, hundreds of feet high. The stream was freefalling straight down into space.

In the fertile valley extending out far below, the stream was but a silvery thin ribbon, with the path, like a faint thread, following along. It continued on its journey through scattered ponds that, from this height, looked like sparkling, blue jewels reflecting the sky, set in a soft green fabric. Trees grew thick at the edges of the valley. From the clouds fell a few wide gray streaks of rain, creating a rainbow—a magical, celestial ornament, hanging in the sky, made of glowing, brilliant, luminous colors.

Auriel pointed to the furthest pond, adjacent to a small cluster of trees. "We'll camp there for the night. Some wild asparagus grows near the pond and tasty fish live in it. We'll ask if any one of them would be willing to be our dinner. If one says "yes," we'll have us a meal that will be the envy of any king!"

It sounded good to Tobe.

The path ran along the edge of the cliff for some distance. The cliff then turned into a steep slope upon which a forest grew, running down to the valley far below. Auriel and Tobe paused before entering.

"Listen," said Auriel. She did not move a muscle.

Below, the wind was creating deep-toned songs in layers as it blew through leaves, needles, and branches of the forest. Tobe could see the wind moving like some giant, invisible serpent, gliding and wending through the whole forest, weaving its way closer and closer up the slope as it sent the branches swaying. Suddenly the tops of the trees looming before Auriel and Tobe bowed, and a burst of air blew upon them with a force that sent their hair flying straight back.

Fascinating! Tobe mused in wonderment.

They started walking again. The trail descended, curving around the trunks of enormous trees, the crowns of which towered high above. It seemed a miracle to Tobe that these colossal giants could grow out of and be sustained by *mere earth*, as if by some unstoppable will. Rocks and roots of trees created well-placed steps along the way—nature's gift to the traveler. The sound of a waterfall was a constant roar, growing louder.

The path came around a large boulder. With a thunderous roar, the massive volume of the waterfall plummeted straight down onto large, unyielding stones. The intense, raging power and force of the scene blasted through Tobe, energizing every part of him, washing him through and through. The waterfall gave rise to swirling, drizzling mists, refreshing Auriel and Tobe. Soft breezes animated the columns of mist, turning them into spirits gliding about, glowing with the colors of a rainbow.

Tobe walked right up to the falls and looked straight up. He watched a single droplet of water free-fall from high above, coming closer and closer. For a moment he felt as if he were that droplet, falling through space and time. Finally, with a kerplunk and little splash, it merged back into the oneness of the pool at the base of the falls. Tobe felt a chill run through his body as he, too, for a second sensed himself merging with *something* bigger than himself.

In this grotto filled with the energy of the falls, Auriel and Tobe rested. In spite of the noise, Auriel took a nap in a dry place under a large rock overhang. Tobe sat, absorbing the scene, as the fresh mist enlivened him.

Auriel awoke after a short spell, and they were soon on the path again. It zigzagged down the hill, now and then crossing over the rushing stream. Giant fallen logs, flattened on top, created small bridges for easy passage. The path suddenly turned a bend, bringing Auriel and Tobe face to face with a man sitting on a large rock.

"Hello there," said the man. "It's nice to see you again, Auriel. It's been way too long."

He turned to Tobe. "My name is Aban. Some here call me the 'Borderland Man.'" He punctuated his statement with a grin. "But you can call me whatever you wish. And who might you be?"

"My name is Tobe."

Aban studied Tobe closely. "What are you two up to? I can see your friend is a stranger here." Tobe started to feel self-conscious.

"We are exploring Inlăkesh," said Auriel. "And Tobe wants to see the River Is."

"Well, you have come to the right place. I was just about to ride the River myself," said Aban.

Tobe's heart beat faster; his enthusiasm mounted.

Auriel turned toward Tobe. "Why don't you two talk? I will meet up with you later."

"That's fine with me," said Aban. Tobe nodded in agreement.

Standing alone before Aban, Tobe said the first thing that came to his mind. "Why do they call you 'the Borderland Man'?"

"Oh, it's because I live on the borderland between worlds—between *Here* and *Everywhere*. No finer line exists anywhere!"

"Have you ever been to *Everywhere*?" Aban asked, continuing to study Tobe closely. "I guess that is a silly question," said Aban before Tobe could reply. "You haven't even ridden the River Is yet." There was a short pause then Aban added, "So you want to see the River, do you?"

"You are right," Tobe answered. I have never been to *Everywhere*, and up until now, I would have thought it quite impossible. And more than anything, I would like to get to know the River."

"Any minute now," said Aban, "the River will come in all Its power and wash me away. Do you want to ride with me?"

Tobe grew nervous. "I would rather get to know the River slowly. You know . . . stick a toe in . . . then the foot, then up to the knees . . . like that." Tobe felt disappointed that he was not braver.

"As you wish. That's one way to do it." Aban anxiously looked around and then up in the sky. He continued. "Sometimes, Tobe, folks don't have a choice. The River just comes in all Its splendor and picks them up and washes them away!"

Aban adjusted his position on the rock. "Let's see; where was I? Oh yes, I was going to say, I ride the River Is over and over, as much as I can. It's what all the folks in these parts do. There is only *joy* in the River. You will see. But take it slowly at first, if you wish."

Aban pointed to some large boulders nestled in the trees a little distance away. "There's good shade there. You will be comfortable. You can watch from there. This shouldn't take long." Aban then looked straight up and in a very calm voice said, "Ah, the River is here. Do you feel It? Go to the rocks and watch."

Tobe walked quickly to the rocks. Turning, he saw Aban still sitting where he had left him. Tobe looked about, but could see no River Is anywhere. He climbed up on the largest bolder to get a better view. He could just make out Aban's face. It had an expression of the deepest calm. Tobe sat there, watched and waited—and watched and waited.

Tobe heard something moving through the bushes, coming closer. He was relieved to see it was Auriel. "I had a feeling I would find you here," she said as she stepped through the last branches. "Are you ready to go? Did you have a good chat with Aban?"

"I'm waiting for the River to wash him away," said Tobe, pointing at Aban sitting on a rock in the distance. "But as you can see, he's still there. He said it would take no time at all, but that was some time ago."

"But the River *has* come," said Auriel. "And he *is* gone. The River *has* whisked him clean away!"

Now, this made no sense at all to Tobe, for he could see him, clear as day.

"Yes, his *body* is there," continued Auriel, "but *he* is swimming in the River. You see, Tobe, you don't need to go anywhere to go to *Everywhere*. Sometimes the body is taken along and sometimes it is left behind."

Tobe was dumbfounded and yet fascinated. There was so much he could neither anticipate nor fathom. *How strange and full of surprises Inlākesh is!*

Auriel and Tobe made their way to the valley floor. By the time they reached the last pond, the sun was already behind the mountains, giving the air a touch of coolness. Tobe took a branch and whittled a point to make a spear. Fishing was in his blood, and he knew how to read a fish. It was not long before he carried a nice-sized one back to the fire Auriel had built. He cleaned the fish and began cooking it on the flames. Tobe had a small pan in his backpack, just big enough for Ariel to cook the asparagus. There was still bread for both of them to enjoy. After their delicious meal, Tobe stretched out on the soft grass and instantly fell asleep.

CHAPTER EIGHT

Swimming in the River Is

. . . whether in the body, or out of the body, I could not tell.
The Bible

To See a World in a Grain of Sand
And a Heaven in a Wild Flower,
Hold Infinity in the palm of your hand
And Eternity in an hour.

William Blake

 CHORUS OF BIRDS AWOKE Tobe. He sat up. It took a few seconds for him to put all the pieces together of who and where he was. He stretched. Never before had he felt so refreshed from a night's sleep. A wave of happiness settled over him, so deep that he barely recognized himself.

He saw Auriel approaching, carrying something in a large handkerchief. "I have some tasty seeds, berries, and leaves, and with the last bit of bread, we will have us a fine and dandy breakfast."

After breakfast, Auriel and Tobe continued their journey through the valley. Then, the trail suddenly began to ascend. The farther up they went, the ground became rockier, with only the occasional tuft of grass and small wildflower. Tobe had to stop a couple times to catch his breath. Higher and higher, the trail continued its steep climb. Tobe was sure that soon he would be able to reach up and touch the clouds.

They came to a dome-shaped peak and scaled to the top. Reaching the crest, an immense landscape opened up below. They were up so high, they could see the curvature of the world. In the vast plain below, mountain ranges, one after another, faded into the horizon, where eyes could see no farther. The sky was gigantic! Tobe had never seen so much sky in one place before! From this height, the world did not appear real at all. The air was so thin and light that Tobe felt at any moment he could be pulled up into it. A hush rested upon everything. Every plant and tree, every rock and mountain peak seemed bathed in contentment.

They sat down to rest on a rock. Nearby ridges covered with trees and meadows meandered willy-nilly down to the plain far below. At the base of the mountain, Tobe could make out the structures of a large village—tiny dashes and dots, all close together. The plain itself had very little vegetation, like a desert land, except for a few, narrow green bands where rivers ran across the plain—water runoff from the mountain ranges.

"At times," said Auriel, "you can actually hear the River Is calling." As her sentence faded away, a soft rumble of thunder rolled through the clouds overhead. *An auspicious sign.*

Auriel paused, taking in the scene. "There is nothing more powerful in this world than the River Is—even though It is invisible and subtler than a whisper. Yet, you *will* see It."

Curious little bright-eyed chipmunks emerged and sat on nearby rocks to look at their guests. The clouds overhead were growing larger and darker. Again, from deep within their folds, came the muted rumble of thunder . . . and again.

"The time has come," said Auriel. "Are you ready to call the River?"

Tobe was taken by surprise. "Yes!" he exclaimed. He felt fear and a resistance suddenly well up inside him.

"You can call the River in different ways . . .," Auriel continued.

Tobe was not listening. Instead, his attention was on what he had just observed within himself. *How can I see the River if I fear It!* He was perplexed and troubled.

"Are you listening?" Auriel was examining Tobe closely.

Auriel's words brought Tobe back to his senses.

"Auriel, I don't know what's going on. Just then, as you spoke of calling the River, I suddenly felt a wall come up. I don't understand."

"Some things you can ignore; some things you *have* to look at," she said. "See what's behind the wall. No doubt a hobgoblin or two . . . made of nothing."

Auriel sat patiently as Tobe took a moment to study his inner world. He was quiet for some time and then said, "There is a feeling that I am not strong enough." Then he saw something deeper. "I am not worthy enough!"

"Hobgoblins for sure!" Auriel smiled, making light of the whole thing. "You are learning how to call the River. Beginnings are often awkward. Look at a baby eaglet when it first learns to fly. It is not so confident either. You will get better at this, Tobe. Patience is what you need now . . . and a little self-forgiveness wouldn't be bad either."

Something small moved near Auriel's feet. She knelt down to investigate it.

"Look at this," said Auriel, pointing near her feet. "Quite a handsome fellow, isn't he?"

A colorful, shiny-shelled insect—iridescent blue and turquoise, with touches of deep emerald green—scurried on the ground. He looked like a king of a miniature land in all his fine apparel. On his feet were what appeared to be brilliant orange socks, all six of them moving as if on some very important business.

Auriel arose and sat back down on the rock. Turning her attention back to Tobe, she said, "You *are* strong. You *are* worthy." Her eyes were warm with feeling. "You cannot see it because you are looking in the wrong place. You are looking in that place that lies to us about what we are. One day you will see that you *are* the strength and purity of the River, Itself. If anything *is* worthy, *you* are, Tobe!"

Once again, Tobe could feel Auriel's words enter him like a healing balm.

"Let's try calling the River now," continued Auriel. "Begin by just acknowledging that It *is* here—*now*. The truth is the River can be found only 'here' and 'now'—free of the past and future. The River flows—and flows from second to second—forever! Go to the *life* of this present second, and you will find the River waiting there.

"Remember when you were in the canyon looking at space," added Auriel, "and you *saw* and *sensed* the very life of space? That, Tobe, was your first little glimpse of the River—a mere hint, but you were not ready, so I did not say more. Now you are ready. Look on space, past form. The River can be seen more clearly there, at least at first. Call It, Tobe."

Again, Tobe was astounded by how simple the truly important things were. Excitedly, he brought his focus on the space that surrounded him and on the present . . . the present second. He directed his attention with a strong determination.

"You are trying too hard," Auriel said. "It's not a breaking through, but a dissolving into. It's more about grace than force. It *is* here! Relax. Just *surrender* into Its living presence, which surrounds you now. Gently melt into It."

Tobe watched as he let go of all the past, along with all his concerns for the future. Right *here*—right *now* was all there was! His gaze softened as he looked upon space, feeling the life of the present second. The is-ness of the moment began to shine with *life*!

"That's it, Tobe. Keep going."

This life grew so strong, flowing everywhere in space, surrounding and bathing all the forms of the landscape—the rocks, plants, and little creatures—Auriel and himself too! It was holding everything in its quiet, yet mighty embrace—in a oneness beyond comprehension. Tobe held his attention upon this *life* and did not let it waver.

"Congratulations, Tobe!" said Auriel. "Do you see what just happened? It is a miracle! *You have just called the River Is, and you are looking at It!*"

Tobe was elated! He had no words to express his excitement. Yes, he could see the River everywhere!

Then, despite his ecstatic state, a feeling that something was missing entered him. He could hear in his mind the call of the cowgirl, "Swim deep in the River." Then he remembered Aban, the Borderland Man, how he was washed away by the power of the River.

"There is more, Auriel. *I need more*! Looking at the River is not enough; I must *swim* in It!"

"I was hoping you would say that. Go ahead," said Auriel, smiling. "It is waiting for you."

Tobe surrendered to the River. It streamed through him, washing him clean through and through. He started to ride Its life like a wave, as It carried him along.

The force of the River amazed him. Yet when he reached out to touch It, his fingers grasped nothing. Tobe could not imagine anything more powerful . . . and yet, more mysteriously subtle.

The changelessness of the River, too, surprised him. Things in the physical were changing all about him—the sounds, fragrances, insects, and animals moving about—all was constantly changing. Yet the River— its peace, its stillness—was constant and never changed!

The River Flowing around Auriel and Tobe

Yet the changelessness in the River was not static. It was unbelievably dynamic. Tobe was traveling through layers of this changeless *life*, with each layer growing deeper and richer, as if through petals in an opening flower. This he saw with eyes that not only could *feel* but now could *see* the *invisible*!

"You can ride the present second to *forever*!" called out Auriel.

The River, flowing around and through things, animated them with a brighter life. In the River, the simplest thing—a pebble, the smallest green shoot, a dewdrop—became a miracle to behold. Up until now, the world was a solid thing, but in the River all forms—rocks, plants, trees, and earth—became pure energy, pure vibration, all cloaked in only the illusion of form, held within the Oneness of the River.

Tobe formed a cup with his hand and dipped it into the River. In his hand, he saw the River there in all Its fullness—whole and complete! It was identical in every way to the boundless River he saw flowing all about him. He *knew* that in his hand, he held the whole River. "Every bit of the River holds the *whole*," he said astounded. "What kind of River is this? A strange, heavenly magic is in It!"

As the River flowed about Tobe, he began to feel himself less and less "in his skin," until he was totally free of his bodily form. He felt transparent—lucid. His spirit expanded. He easily swam past the outer surface of things and entered into their very life. And all things rejoiced to be *known*!

As Tobe continued swimming in the River, he looked over and was astounded to see his body now walking down the path, talking to Auriel! Tobe had never seen such a peculiar sight. *So it is possible to do one thing, while the body is doing something else!*

The River faded away, and just like that, Tobe was walking down the trail, next to Auriel. All concepts of what he had thought the River would be were completely washed away, yet what It *was* he could not comprehend.

"You look magnificent in the River," Auriel said.

Tobe looked at her and gratitude filled him. He realized how fortunate he was to have this "child" as his guide. "Thank you," said Tobe, "for everything."

Then a stone caught Tobe's eye. He reached down and picked it up, studying its weight and quality. Next, his attention drifted to a bush. He ran his fingers along one of its branches. He was amazed at how "solid" the stone and branch felt to his fingers, after having just seen in the River how all things are pure energy, with only the illusion of solidity. And the fact that he now thought it "amazing" seemed even more *amazing*!

Time lightly passed as they made their descent down the ridge. To Tobe, it did not matter which way they were going, for as he had seen, the River was *everywhere*.

As they walked, they entered a grove of trees. Tobe felt a hush come over him, as if he were entering a sacred place. They both paused. It felt as if they were standing in a cathedral, but it was not a place made with hands. It had no chiseled stone columns, nor marble-tiled floors. Its floor was a carpet of fallen leaves, thick upon the ground, its fragrance filling the air like incense.

The large trunks of trees were the columns of this cathedral—holding up a green, arched ceiling high above. The stones in the cathedral seemed alive. Erect and upright, they stood like statues of saints. There was a large one for an altar, and a few smaller ones for sitting.

The sun beamed down through the branches, its mottled light adorning the forest floor. The light shone through the red, yellow, and blue petals of blossoms and the green leaves of plants, turning them aglow like light through stained glass. A deep soft thunder echoed through the clouds above—a rumbling benediction from the Heavens.

It seemed the moment held its breath and stood still as it entered into timelessness. Then Auriel and Tobe exited the grove from the other side.

Auriel, overcome by joy, started playfully skipping down the path. Then laughing, with arms extended, she began to spin—and after a few twirls, ended up in a walking gait, motioning to Tobe to catch up.

The whole area was in shadow now, as the storm gained in its advance. As they walked, the path made a sharp turn, opening to a scene that pierced Tobe like a knife. Mighty, fierce flames were consuming the whole forest on an adjacent ridge. It was close enough that Tobe could make out individual trees, large and majestic, being consumed by the immense flames. He felt a deep sense of sorrow as he watched. He could do nothing; he had never known devastation on such a scale.

"Lightning," said Auriel.

With anxiety in his voice, Tobe said, "How could this be happening? Inlăkesh seems like such a perfect place."

"Destruction will always be a part of the natural world as *we* see it," said Auriel.

They stood there silently for a few moments.

"But does it have to be that way?" Tobe asked.

Auriel responded, "Destruction touches the entire universe. Even whole galaxies are destroyed. But it is a dream of destruction—a dream of death. *It is no more real than that. In the River, nothing is lost.* There, life is constant and eternal.

"As you look on such things," continued Auriel, "remember that what truly lives, does not die. The forms go; that is all. Things are not at all the way they seem."

The scene held Tobe's gaze transfixed. The words, "There is no death," kept repeating in his mind. As he watched, the scene began to change.

"It's about letting go," Auriel said. "Let the trees teach you, Tobe. Hold onto *nothing.*"

They continued to watch the fire in silence. Then Auriel lightly touched Tobe. "Come on. I want you to experience something in the village."

Words started stirring in Tobe. "Wait. Give me a moment, Auriel." Tobe took out a pencil and started jotting down words. This is what he wrote:

A True Tree Tale

The father tree and the child tree were standing on the hill, as they always had, their needles glistening in the wind. Up above, against the purest blue sky, a silent parade of clouds, glowing white, glided peacefully by.

After a while, the child tree noticed something strange. "What is that, Father? There is something different in the air."

The father tree was silent for a moment, sensing the air, now blowing strong from the west.

"Yes, you are right, Son." His voice was more serious than the child tree had ever heard before. "Today is the day . . .," The father tree seemed to be choosing his words carefully, "the day many of us have been waiting for, for a long time."

"Why . . . what is happening, Father?"

"We stopped here to rest a spell, a long time ago, and now we are going home. We are going to fly today, my Son."

"But how? We have no wings," said the child tree.

"Our wings will come to us. They are full of life and energy, and they will free our feet from the ground."

"Are our wings made of feathers, Father, like the birds' that make their nests in our branches?"

The father tree did not have time to reply, for just at that instant, cascading over the crest of the hill came a giant wave of gray smoke so thick the trees could hardly breathe. Behind the smoke, an army of galloping, leaping flames charged. The forest fell silent.

The child tree saw even the wisest, most ancient trees shaking before the flames.

"I am afraid, Father!"

"There is no reason to be, my Son. The trees do not quake with fear. It is but the wind of the firestorm. Look again, and see how brave, noble, and strong our family stands; how beautiful they are in form and courage. There is no death. You will see. Hold my hand tight; you will be fine, my Son."

The flames drew closer and began licking all about. They jumped upon the trunks of the father tree and the child tree, where the flames grew bold and strong. Sparks, flying in the air, landed in their evergreen crowns, sending them ablaze.

Above the noise of the crackling flames, the child tree could hear his beloved father's voice, "Have courage, Son. There is no death. The flames are our wings. It is time, my Son, to fly. I love you so."

Tobe finished, folded up the paper, put it in his pocket, and on they went. As they walked, Auriel asked, "Do you feel the River now?"

"No. It faded away."

Auriel's expression became serious. "You're wrong. It is not called the 'River *Was*.' It's the River *Is* and *always IS*! Look, the River is here, right now. It flows all about you still. It faded only from your awareness, that is all."

Tobe felt uncomfortable. An awkward smile came to his face. "I guess I got distracted."

"Your inattention," said Auriel, "caused many wondrous things to slip through your fingers. Don't feel bad about it. Just observe that is what happened. The day will come, though, when you hold onto the River as if your next breath, your very life depended on it. Just walking around, distracted by the world, will no longer be enough for you."

Tobe knew that Auriel was right; things *were* different now. To be lackadaisical had a price. Tobe determined to be more vigilant, and he would start right *now* by calling the River.

He looked to the changeless *life* in the moment and kept his gaze there. He could feel the force of the River approaching, getting stronger . . . and stronger . . ., until it was like a silent ROAR!

"The River is growing mighty!" he exclaimed.

This was the last thing Tobe said before the most unexpected thing happened. Fear, once again, rose up and overtook him as the intensity of the River grew. Instantly, the River withdrew.

Tobe stood there, disheartened, and a touch ashamed. He sighed, "Oh, Auriel, I hesitated before the power of the River. There I was as It approached, and fear overcame me again. Now I cannot see It."

"Yes, the River reveals itself where the heart is open and where It is welcomed—" said Auriel.

"Yet I have been in the River!" Tobe interrupted. "I have seen Its beauty! How could I fear it? I just don't understand why . . ." With jaw hard set and self-loathing burning in his eyes, he shook his head in disbelief as he plopped down on a large fallen log.

Then looking around, as if speaking to the River, Tobe said, "Take me, kicking and screaming if it must be so. Is not this one, sincere wish—this one, earnest prayer enough?!"

As she sat next to Tobe, Auriel said, "You rode in the River one moment and were afraid of It the next." In her voice, Tobe could hear no trace of judgment. "We are always fluctuating. The only time we are ever truly consistent is when we are in the River.

"Fear is natural," she continued. "It is natural to hesitate before the unknown. Fear keeps us locked up within ourselves—separate from each other and from what we really are. Fear works better than sturdy prison bars and vigilant jailers. Nevertheless, fear is insubstantial and made of nothing. It is a game we play on ourselves. Don't be too hard on yourself. I know you have courage."

Auriel paused for a moment, leaned slightly closer, and spoke with emphasis, "Do you want to know the greatest trick we play on ourselves? Before you came to this world, you were a master rider of the River Is!"

Auriel's words instantly hit some vague cord of memory deep within Tobe—beyond his conscious mind. *A master rider of the River Is*, he repeated to himself, contemplating every word—letting the words call out for a distant memory to come.

"You, who were once free and one with the River," continued Auriel, "then dreamed yourself a body—in a dream of a world. So small, limited, and vulnerable is this dream of yourself that it is hard for you to even hear what I am saying. Yet, you could remember now if you weren't afraid of your very own grandeur." Auriel gave Tobe some space to let the words sink in.

As they started walking again, Auriel said, "The River is everyone's eternal home. You have forgotten so much since you left It to be born in Soñadora, as has everyone else there. You are finally just returning home—that's all. And a part of you knows it.

"So you see what a trick this fear plays on us? Don't take it so seriously, and you'll be fine. Soon this fear will be gone forever. Go swim in the River, Tobe, and know once again what you *really* are."

Auriel's words lifted Tobe's spirits. He found his fears and anxiety mysteriously evaporating away into thin air. Again, he felt strong within himself. He was ready.

He called the River. In an instant, It was all about them. This time, he calmly watched as It grew stronger . . . and stronger. He dove in and rode the current.

It was different this time. The deeper he swam, the more his heart opened. The River rushed in, making his heart like new, washing away the deep-seated roots of fear and suffering. Stillness filled him. Thoughts, sensations, and feelings were still arising within him, but now they did not touch him. They were like little clouds, peacefully floating by.

He could observe that the River was made of a crystal-clear awareness—an awareness full of seeing, unlimited in scope. Tobe watched and marveled as it flowed inside of him, blending with his own awareness—transforming his inner world to pure seeing. It was *that* which now looked out of his eyes!

The River carried him beyond himself. He was becoming larger and larger as he spread throughout the River. As he swam, it became difficult for him to tell where he ended and the River began. Nothing could define him now, yet *everything* did.

"Oh, sweet River," he murmured, "You are *My Self*!"

Tobe was astonished as the River and he flowed beyond Inlăkesh and then beyond the world altogether—becoming pure, vast radiance! The world could not contain the River or Tobe. When Tobe again turned his focus back upon the world, it appeared like a jewel in a dimension of its own! As he looked, he could see the radiance of the River shining through all the forms of the world, like light in a kaleidoscope, shining through the moving colored chips of glass, transforming them to glowing. Now the world was even more mysterious—and even more beautiful to behold!

CHAPTER NINE

Bobbers and Love
in the River Is

It is Love that holds everything together, and is everything.
Rumi

 OBE WAS EXCITED AND turned to Auriel, saying, "I've writ-
ten a poem, Auriel. Listen:

"What joy!

        The River Is ran

                And I swam.

     O, to do it

        Agan

             and

               Agan!"

Auriel laughed in shared delight. "That's good!" Tobe handed the poem
to her and she glanced it over. "And you even left the small 'i' out—the only
way to swim in the River!"

Tobe had no idea what Auriel meant, but he was thrilled that someone
finally *really* liked one of his poems.

Auriel and Tobe walked slowly; they were in no hurry. The brook now flowed strong among boulders in its steep decline down the ridge. The path and brook continued to dance side by side, occasionally crisscrossing each other, falling serpentine-like, down to the valley floor. As they continued, large trees slowly started to give way to smaller evergreens, round and bulbous looking. The ground became more barren too. The delicate, soft, leafy plants of the forest gave way to heartier, more stubborn-looking ones, made to survive in a dryer land.

Auriel and Tobe stopped to rest and they heard the sound of voices from behind. Coming down the path was the family they had seen yesterday, returning from their excursion. Again, everyone shared warm greetings in passing. This time Tobe saw them differently. Their smiles had such warmth to them. Looking into their eyes, he saw the infinite depth of their being, shining with a clear, calm, lucid light.

After they walked by, Tobe asked Auriel, "Did you see how magnificent they looked? Did you feel the very miracle of their existence?"

"You are starting to live in a new world, and see with new eyes," replied Auriel.

As they reached the valley floor, Tobe saw a man standing on a sandbank on the edge of the stream, with a fishing pole in hand. The man cast out a line. The bait and bobber splashed on the surface of the water, the bobber floating downstream in the current.

Tobe went to speak to the fisherman. "Having any luck?" he asked.

The fisherman, intensely focused on his bobber, acknowledged Tobe with a nod. "Not yet. But I am fishing for The Great Fish—and that *is* already good luck!"

When the man mentioned "The Great Fish," Tobe's heart quickened. Instantly he remembered the poet's book and his love for The Great Fish. Tobe had completely forgotten about The Great Fish. Until now, he was not even sure It really existed, thinking perhaps It was nothing more than a poet's metaphor.

"You expect to find The Great Fish in this little stream?" Tobe asked.

"Oh goodness, no!" said the fisherman. "I'm not fishing that itty bitty brook; I am fishing in the River Is."

Now, that made perfect sense to Tobe. He silently watched the fisherman for a while and then said, "Would you mind telling me what you know about The Great Fish and the tricks of catching It? I might want to try my hand at it."

Tobe's request brought a smile to the fisherman. "There is no other subject I would rather talk about," he said, reeling in the line a bit and then letting it out again. "Sometimes The Great Fish only nibbles at the bait, creating mere ripples on the surface of the River Is. Then come those magical times when It strikes the bait with all Its might and runs with it! Then I am pulled into the River, pole and all. What a ride! Deep into the River we go!

"But it always happens that The Great Fish, after a moment or two, spits out the hook and goes on Its merry way. Then I shoot back up to the surface of the River Is and swim back to the shore. Then, as soon as I can, I bait the hook, cast it out, and wait once again."

The fisherman glanced at Tobe and then promptly returned his attention to his bobber. "I tell you," continued the fisherman, "once you feel the power of That Fish as it strikes and catch a glimpse of Its magnificent size, *you* will be the one that is 'hooked.' And you will spend the rest of your life fishing for That Fish!"

"I am a fisherman too," said Tobe, "but nothing as extraordinary as fishing for The Great Fish. Back home, we only catch the golden minnow, which you can hold in the palm of your hand with no problem at all. You are a whole different kind of fisherman."

The fisherman suddenly became anxious as his line jerked taught. There was a moment of tense silence.

"Never mind. It was nothing," said the Fisherman. "Anyway . . . what were you saying?"

"What is it you use for bait?" Tobe asked.

"Ah, a very good question. If only people would ask more questions like that." The fisherman reeled in the line a bit and let it out again. "The bait that works best is to take a hand full of 'longing' and tie it neatly on the hook with little threads of 'awareness.' In stormy weather, I particularly like to braid 'prayers' together on the hook. Once cast out, they dangle nicely in the River."

The fisherman studied Tobe a little more closely and again returned his attention to the bobber. "You smile. Don't you believe it possible to catch The Great Fish with such bait? Surely you don't think It would eat worms, do you?" The fisherman chuckled aloud. "Oh, you misunderstand it all anyway. You can't really catch The Great Fish," he said, still chuckling. "It's quite impossible, really. *It* catches *you*."

Tobe could tell that the fisherman was a master of this sport.

"I would like to fish with you someday," said Tobe.

"That would be my pleasure. Come any day. This is where I will be."

"Well, it's been very . . . nice." Tobe could not believe how empty the word "nice" was, compared to the excitement he felt when speaking to the fisherman about The Great Fish.

"I hope to see you again soon," said the fisherman.

Tobe smiled, turned, and walked toward Auriel. As he walked, he thought of better words he could have used instead of "nice," like "astonishing!," "spectacular!," "utterly fantastic!"—any of those words would have done just fine.

Auriel and Tobe had not gone far when they heard the sound of an incredible splash. Tobe turned to look. He could see the River Is clearly, and giant ripples moved on Its surface, but nowhere was the fisherman to be seen.

Tobe wondered how all this could be real. *Am I dreaming?* The question echoed in his mind.

On the plain of the valley floor, the path now became a wide lane. Along the lane were wood fences and short walls of stone. The stream ran parallel, its rhythmic gurgling song rising from the throats of stones. Large trees grew along its banks, setting the lane in deep, cool shadow. The water of the stream irrigated the farmlands beyond, giving life to orchards, fields of crops, and meadows. Cows and horses contentedly grazed, some casting inquisitive glances at Auriel and Tobe as they passed.

"Soon," said Auriel, "we will be coming to the village. It is called Góndāwă. It is an old name meaning 'The Happy Place.' You will get a closer look at how those in Inlăkesh live and what they are like. More importantly, you will learn to swim in the River with others."

As Auriel and Tobe got nearer, Tobe could see that the dwellings made of earth harmoniously rose from the ground and rested upon it. The quaint charm of the homes, with everything in its place, spoke of caring and attention to detail. People could be seen tending their fields and animals, their conversations rising in pleasant tones and then fading away again.

People appeared, walking in the lane. As they passed, they greeted Auriel and Tobe. The people looked completely at ease. Tobe saw no defense or fear in them, and their eyes seemed to bless him as they passed.

Tobe felt an irresistible urge to draw. He turned toward Auriel and said, "I would like to draw the River Is . . . here, in this place. Do you think it can be done? I cannot think of a greater subject. Can you, Auriel?"

"I think it's a splendid idea," she said. "I don't see how you can miss!"

Tobe, excited at this new challenge, quickly took off his backpack and got out his brushes, colored pencils, sketchbook, and paints. Auriel joined Tobe on a large rock where she could watch.

Since Tobe was already standing in the River, he didn't need to call It. He took a moment to study It though, as an artist studies things. Then, out of his backpack, he pulled a simple piece of black paper. He held it out, musing over its deep, rich blackness.

"Here, Auriel, look at this paper; its blackness . . . the deepest essence of the River Is, beyond all form. Do you see how still It is? Do you feel Its bottomless peace?" He smiled in wonderment at the simplicity of truth.

"Amazing, like magic," said Auriel. "The black paper says it perfectly. And you haven't even done anything yet!"

On his palette, Tobe squeezed out a splotch of gold paint from a tube. In two wide, bold, wavy strokes he brushed on the iridescent gold, all glittery against the deep black of the paper.

"Ah, there. . . . That expresses It even better—the radiant, ever-flowing life of the River Is in all Its glory!" said Tobe, in awe at how simple it was to paint the incomprehensible River in just a couple strokes. Auriel seemed impressed too.

Tobe grew still as he looked upon the River's splendor. In firm vertical lines, he drew Its will and power. He drew Its clear, conscious energy with wavy lines, with curlicues, and dancing specs of energy, changing colors as he went; and he drew the peace of the River in horizontal lines— with a slow and gentle hand. Next, he started painting the River flowing around and through everything, with washes of color—turquoise, purple, and blue—all transparent.

Then, with a light hand, Tobe started drawing the forms of the world— clouds, birds, mountains and mesas, trees, a stable and farmhouse, horses in the meadow with ducks, and someone tending their garden. He painted them with colors, transparent here and there, the way they seem to be, now and then, when one is swimming in the River.

By now, the rendering of the forms of the world covered over much of the River. So Tobe redrew some zigzags, curlicues, and a few lines, wavy as well as straight, to make the River clear once again. *The real subject, after all, is the River!* Tobe told himself.

Then at the top he brushed on white paint with a touch of yellow to give it warmth. As he painted, the thoughts came, *Ah, the light that flows in the River—the light that is within and animates all things.* He brushed it on, radiant and glowing. The image now felt complete. The creation of the picture came effortlessly, for the River was guiding Tobe's heart and hand.

Tobe chuckled. Back in Soñadora, no one would appreciate such squiggles and strokes, and they might even think him mad, but that did not matter. He knew that every creature in Inlăkesh would instantly recognize and appreciate a portrait of what they all knew and loved so well.

So something happened that day that had never, ever happened before in Inlăkesh. Our unpretentious, simple Tobe, with his modest skill, sitting on a rock with pencil and brush in hand, drew the great River Is. He drew It in all Its beauty and power; and he painted It flowing in Inlăkesh and beyond this dimension altogether!

Auriel glanced over the picture. "It's beautiful. You captured it! How wonderful!"

Tobe was overjoyed. "It's yours."

Tobe's Painting of the River Is and the World.
"O beautiful world, O glorious world—full of sublime mystery, overflowing with Love—all held in the Oneness of the River." (Tobe)

"Thank you, Tobe, but you better keep it to remember this day."

Sitting silently, she continued studying it while Tobe packed up. "The River belongs to you now," said Auriel, "and *you* belong to It. I can see you love It . . . almost as much as It loves you."

"To be in the River and draw It at the same time is wonderful." Tobe said, "What is strange is that, before, I could not even see the River, but now It is so obvious. I breathe It. I move in It. My very being floats in It!"

Auriel smiled, "Don't you want to go for a swim to celebrate your 'masterpiece?'"

Tobe nodded, "Good idea."

He closed his eyes and surrendered deeper into the River. He felt like sugar dissolving into water. He started to sense, even more, the *life* of the River. A deep peace and happiness started to fill him. He was amazed at how the River carried him along lovingly. *It flows with Love!* The Love became more real as Tobe swam along. He realized, as water is to a river, *Love* is to the River Is!

"Surrender *everything* to the River," Auriel called out. "Its Love will hold you."

Tobe relaxed and surrendered completely and let the current carry him. As he opened his eyes and looked about at the landscape, he saw everything bathed in Love.

Tobe looked at a leaf falling from a tree—its arch and sway as it fell was Love's dancing. The leaf's gentle landing upon the ground was Love's light touch. The path that Auriel and Tobe had traveled along was Love, and the shade that rested upon it from the tree branches above, that was Love's gift of cool comfort. The sun's life-giving light—that, too, was Love's gift.

Love was everywhere Tobe looked, for the Love of the River had flowed into him and was looking out of his eyes. As Tobe swam deeper, he was astonished to discover that there was no difference in this Love and what he was! He realized he was expanding—as big as Love itself.

It was then, for the first time, that Tobe heard the song that each and every rock, every green growing thing, nurturing earth, generous sky, and creatures all around had been singing all along, but which, until now, he could not hear. It was their constant song of Love, in gratitude, to the River Is, for Its Love for them.

As Tobe floated in the River, a feeling welled up inside him that grew so strong that he could not keep it in. "O, River—*My Self,* you are true Happiness, true Joy," he sighed, "How I do love you, sweet River!"

CHAPTER TEN

The Village of Góndāwă

O, wonder! How many goodly creatures are there here!
How beauteous mankind is! O, brave new world, that has
such people in't!

William Shakespeare

VENTUALLY, TOBE'S SWIM CAME to an end. Everything seemed perfect. All was going so well. His heart had never felt lighter. He was relaxed—but too relaxed. He was beaming with confidence—but with too much confidence. Tobe had forgotten one necessary thing: to be mindful. He hadn't gone beyond the need for that yet. With Auriel by his side, they headed toward the village.

Then something strange started happening. One single, simple, dark thought came into Tobe's mind. He quickly brushed it aside, seeing it as no more than a pesky little thing. Then, without him noticing, tiptoeing in came another and then another. They kept coming. They became louder and louder in his mind.

"Who do you think you are anyway?" said one.

"You are all show—all pretense," said another.

"You think you are so great, but you are worthless."

Without him noticing, he started listening to their dreary, dismal mutterings. On and on they came. They grew darker—full of self-loathing and doubt. These thoughts were even judging Auriel. Piling atop each other, these thoughts grew large, casting a long, dark shadow across Tobe's heart and inner world.

"I feel most peculiar . . .," Tobe said, as he turned to Auriel.

He paused. She was not there! He could not see her anywhere!

"Auriel, where are you?" he called out.

No answer came.

It all happened so quickly. Feeling dazed, Tobe was completely under the spell of these thoughts. He looked around. He could no longer see the light of Inlăkesh in the world. He found himself instead in the darkness of what seemed like a different world completely.

Everything felt heavy, threatening. Fear now tore and ravaged Tobe's inner world. No longer on a firm foundation, he was sent reeling in utter panic—carried away, like a feather in a breeze, sucked into another dark hole! And he was too far in to climb back out.

He was reassured by seeing the village ahead. His pace quickened. But upon entering the village, to his horror, he felt instantly vulnerable, with danger lurking about. The people in the village had a coldness in their eyes. Most of them were scurrying around, appearing anxious or upset. Tobe's heart was a wild hammer, its strong blows reverberating throughout his body. *Where am I?* His confusion grew.

Fighting against his fear, he approached a man on the corner and asked, "Am I in Inlăkesh? This is the village Góndăwă, isn't it?"

The man looked at Tobe with disdain. "Are you insane? 'Inlăkesh'? 'Góndăwă'? Sounds like something out of some mad tale." He turned and spit.

Tobe hurried away. *How is it possible to fall from a world so high, to one so low—so quick?*

Tobe did not know it, but the dark hole into which he had fallen was like a portal. Tobe was no longer in the dimension of Inlăkesh.

He felt desperate. "Help me, Auriel!" he called out. His only answer was the berating glances from those who passed.

Tobe desperately struggled to make his way to a place where he could be alone. He plopped down on a stone wall and closed his eyes, hoping that in the darkness, behind closed eyelids, this strange world might go away. He took a few deep breaths. Minutes passed as his heart continued to pound.

Tobe heard a voice in his head, at first barely audible. He strained to hear it. It repeated itself. It was a voice he knew. "Look past your fear, Tobe, straight into the darkness." It was Auriel's voice. "See the darkness for what it is. Whatever you do, don't feed the darkness your fear, or it will grow."

In spite of his anxiety, Tobe forced himself to look on his inner world. He mustered all his might and steadied his gaze.

As he looked, he saw how weak all his disparaging thoughts were. They blended with his body sensations, creating a feeling of a "me." It was a *lie* of who he was—broken and forlorn, full of fear. Yes, a *lie*! For he had seen himself in the River and he now knew what he really was.

He had just enough strength to let flames burn up this dark, suffering 'self.' The flames felt soothing. He let go completely, not caring what remained, trusting that what was needed would still be there. He felt relief. He felt lighter and lighter.

"The River is all about you," the voice of Auriel said. "Call It to your awareness and *become* the River, Tobe!"

Tobe tried to remember the different ways to call the River. At first nothing came, his mind impaired by the darkness. He kept trying to remember. *It should be simple. Why is it so hard to remember?!*

Then he remembered to look at what does not change. He opened his eyes. As he focused he began to sense the changeless life all about him, dim at first, growing stronger. As Its peace and oneness began to dawn in his awareness the darkness withdrew like the fog of night before the light and warmth of the morning sun. Finally, the living River was flowing clear in his sight again. Tobe gathered strength from Its touch. Its power flowed into him, instantly becoming his.

Tobe found himself sitting there, alone and spent. Yet he also felt exhilarated, for the power of the River was in him now, and he knew beyond a doubt that no darkness could touch him.

Tobe watched as the village and people started shifting and transforming before his sight. The heaviness fell from all things, and a glow returned. A sense of wonder gently held the world again. He was in the peace of Inlākesh once more.

With a deep sigh of relief, Tobe watched as the last residue of his fear evaporated completely away. He looked around. The surrounding hills cradled the village like a caring mother, and the songs of birds filled the air. He stood and started walking.

The village was more enchanting than he could have ever imagined. Fountains of sparkling, cascading water were singing their splashing song. Trees were in abundance, offering their generous shade, and flowers in pots and hanging baskets were everywhere, their dazzling hues more radiant and pure than any color Tobe could squeeze from a tube.

The pace of life in the village was like a calm, deep breath. The people had a look of tranquility. Some were working, their actions full of care; some were strolling leisurely; some were sitting on park benches, while others were playing a game of kickball. The soft sound of voices filled the air, babbling like a brook, with laughter now and then rising to a crescendo.

Musicians with string and wind instruments played their melodies on street corners. The love of music went deep in Tobe. He stopped for a spell to listen to one playing a flute. The notes rose with ease from the musician's gifted hands and breath. Tobe's inner world fell silent as these notes—these "honored guests"—gracefully entered him, creating inner landscapes of pure emotion.

What a strange and powerful language this is, Tobe mused. *Is there any other form of communication quite like it in the world? The notes are pure energy: totally free of form as they fly! They are barely in this world of solid things at all, and yet what profound effects they have!*

Tobe listened for a little while longer. He then turned, walked a short distance, and sat down on a bench in the shade of a tree. He continued to observe the people in the village. *How they love to laugh together!*

Tobe sensed that here, contentment grew upon contentment, and nothing could enter and disturb the tranquility. Everyone felt this serenity and moved within it.

A light touch on Tobe's shoulder broke his musing

"Hi there, my friend."

Tobe turned. "Auriel! I missed you!"

"I'm sorry things got a little rough for you," said Auriel. "I wasn't sure how long you would be gone. Losing a whole world is no small matter—especially a glorious one like this."

"It is so good to be back . . . and to see you again," said Tobe, ecstatically.

"I'm glad you are back too," said Auriel. "The trickster part of your mind was up to no good, but it caused no real damage from what I can see." She looked him over carefully. "Your mind is powerful, Tobe. You can create amazing things as well as scary things, with no problem at all. These dark things are mere mental vapors weaving illusions—nothing more than that. A good thing, too, or you might still be missing."

"That other world was . . .," Tobe's thoughts trailed off. His attention returned to the village. "This is a beautiful place." They sat there silently.

Tobe noticed that something was different. The impressions of Inlăkesh now entered him more freely. It was as if the suffering of the dark hole had made an open wound, through which impressions now could more freely enter.

"Your heart used to be hard with a false self-confidence," said Auriel, as if knowing what Tobe was going through.

Tobe nodded.

"These dark holes can be your ally," continued Auriel. "Besides making you open and more sincere, they also give you the will to change.

"You have no idea how important this is. If you have it 'all together,' why would you want to move from where you are? You have seen how this 'Tobe,' this 'me' you are experiencing now, is like a house of cards, sometimes swaying back and forth—unstable, unpredictable. It only takes a slight breeze to make it all come toppling down."

"You know you cannot stay there," added Auriel. "It offers no safety. You are becoming more willing to let go and realize your true nature in the River—your true Self."

They fell silent again as they basked in the impressions of Góndāwă. After a few moments Tobe said, "It is so like heaven here. I never thought it possible that this much goodness could exist in one place." His expression became more playful. "This place seems so light that I would not be surprised if at any moment everything would just lift off and float away!"

Auriel grinned, adding, "And do you see how focused everyone appears and how clear their eyes are? They are in touch with something deep in themselves. Yet the people here are the *same* as people everywhere. The only difference is the River. Speaking of which, this would be a good time to learn how to swim with others. And this is how to do it: Just see the River flowing around and through everyone, which It is. Acknowledge them in the River."

Tobe's curiosity was growing. Every time he swam in the River, he learned something new and incredible, and this sounded very different. And it sounded simple. Tobe was liking simple. The greatest, most important things arise out of it.

Tobe took a moment and imagined the River flowing around everyone he saw in the village. He imagined their beings swimming in It. In Góndāwă, that was easy to do, for they *were* swimming in the River—*and they knew it*. Tobe found he got better at imagining it the longer he tried.

He gently moved beyond his body, dove in, and began to swim. It was not long before he noticed he was not alone. He could sense someone else's presence in the River. This being spread large before Tobe's vision. How wonderful it appeared—living energy, awake and conscious, with some kind of clear intelligence to it that Tobe could not quite fathom.

As that formless being came closer to Tobe, they both began spinning and blending together! It was a new way of communicating, a new way of "knowing" another, which Tobe had never experienced before.

When they separated, Tobe joyfully swam on. Then, after a while, someone else appeared, and then another. With each being he spun, often while observing their bodies standing on the bank of the River Is, a little distance away.

As Tobe dove deeper in the River, he looked upon another being swimming there. Suddenly he saw that that person's being was *identical* to his own—identical in such deep and profound ways. As he perceived this *sameness*, Tobe's being instantly merged into a Oneness with them, for there were no longer any distinctions or differences to keep Tobe separate and apart from them! This Oneness then seemed to expand, and how many beings were in this Oneness, Tobe could not tell.

How strange is this thing we call "Individuality" or "Identity," Tobe mused. *How it can shift and transform. As it freely gives itself up, it becomes something so large. It grows more transparent and empty, as it includes more and more within itself—ever One with others and everything—a mystery of sublime subtleness!*

Tobe was suddenly back on the bench, completely refreshed from his swim.

"I see you had a good swim," Auriel said. "It's amazing, isn't it? The River is *your* life . . . and it is a life you *share* with others."

Tobe looked around at the people in the village and felt a deepening affinity with them. He was moving beyond the self-centered, self-referential life. *Each* and *every* person was becoming as important as he was. This realization he experienced not as a loss, but as a gain—for *real* freedom was in it.

"Everyone is so glorious in the River!" said Tobe. "The deeper I swim, the more glorious they are . . . and yet, and this is the most curious part: strangely, though we are unique, we are the *same!*"

"You have just alluded to one of the River's greatest enigmas," said Auriel. "And more importantly, you have *lived* it! You have gone to the heart of the River and the heart of Inlăkesh."

Tobe paused in thought. "Auriel, I know so much more now. Yet the deeper I go in the River, I truly understand less and less!"

"That's a good sign. You are brave, Tobe. You do not understand, and yet you still dive in." Auriel stood. "Come, the day is getting on. The sun will soon set."

Tobe's Sketch of Swimming with Someone in the River.
"Wonder upon wonder! Individuation of Being in dynamic, energetic
interaction!—within and of Oneness Itself!! O wonder upon wonder!"
(Tobe)

They walked down the main lane, which led them out of the village into the countryside beyond. The lane of stone turned into a dirt road. Shadows now stretched across the landscape, growing longer.

After the last farm, the irrigated fields gave way to wild meadows and trees, the dirt road became a path. At the base of a hill, Auriel began to climb quickly.

"Come, Tobe. Let's get to the top before the sunset is completely gone."

Tobe followed quickly behind. When they reached the top, they both were out of breath. They found themselves standing in a large clearing, with views all around. Auriel sat on a rock and Tobe sat next to her. They first faced in the direction of the sun, which was setting behind a mountain range. Tobe watched as it slipped behind the peaks.

An array of clouds filled the sky—wisps, tufts, and curly dabs, like happy, carefree brush strokes across the sky. With the setting sun, the clouds began to come alive with the color of radiant gold. Then their hue shifted to a fiery orange, and finally to a deep rose blush. Then, all the color of the clouds seemed to sigh and surrender their hue to a ghostly gray and the coming of the night.

Tobe turned in the opposite direction, toward the village, visible at the base of a another mountain range. He relished the last bits of glowing light upon its peaks. He looked to the highest point. It was there where he first learned how to call the River. He marveled at how far they had traveled. That was one odd thing about Inlăkesh. It seemed possible to cover large distances quickly and with little strain. He realized it had been a long day—a very wonderful, long day.

He started thinking how time, too, was strange in Inlăkesh. It seemed to freely stretch and expand, like something pliable—sometimes slowing down to almost standing still. Stranger yet, in the River Is, there were times when there was no time at all!

Tobe thought how different time was in Soñadora. There, time lay heavily upon the place. There, everyone was in a hurry, as if time had to be quickly used up before it ran out. Yet in Inlăkesh, time was gentle and rested lightly upon everything.

Lights started to appear in the village of Góndăwă, mere specs in the distance—on street corners, from porches, and from the windows of homes. People were beginning to settle into the night.

Tobe started wondering about their lives. "Surely they suffer," he said to Auriel. "There must be moments of loss or moments when life is just too much. They can't always be so happy . . . so content."

"Yes, of course," Auriel replied. "At times things fail and do not go according to plan. Deep loss comes, along with pain and tears. That, too, is the nature of things. Nevertheless, the people of Góndāwă hold on to the things of this world lightly—even through apparent tragedy and loss. They embrace their sorrow, knowing that at any moment it can blossom into some form of unexpected beneficence.

"They know that all things will fade away in time. Life to them is like a dance—a beautiful dance, in a holy world—to be enjoyed and then let go of. This understanding goes deep into them and never leaves them. In any case, how could a world bathed in the River Is ever grow heavy for long?"

Auriel and Tobe fell silent as they looked into the evening sky. How quickly it had changed. The clouds, now mere gray wisps, were beginning to dissolve away altogether. The faintest hint of radiant blue lingered above the mountains. Tobe saw his first star. As he looked upon it, he was overcome by the beauty of its delicate glittering. He smiled. He felt like he was looking upon an old, dear friend.

After a few moments, another star appeared off to its side. Then Tobe saw another and another—all tiny, precious, sparkling jewels of light. The warm blue glow of the evening sky continued to fade, taking on the darker shade of night. The miracle of a vast multitude of stars slowly began to emerge right before Tobe's eyes. Across part of the sky was a band of stars so dense that it looked like the haze of a soft cloud. Tobe tried to sense the depth of space—the incredible distances between the stars; it was so vast it boggled his mind.

The perfect calmness of the sky was broken now and then by a shooting star, as it became brighter and brighter, and then burned out. All was quiet except for the infrequent hooting of an owl and the rhythmic cadence of crickets, their sound harmonizing perfectly with the twinkling of the stars.

To Tobe, this breathtaking vision of the grandeur of the universe seemed like something that should be reserved for saints and the most holy ones, and even then, only after years of the most arduous dedication. Yet here it was: *freely* held out for *all* to look upon—even a simple, ordinary person like himself! A wave of gratitude overwhelmed him as he looked upon this most astonishing gift.

Auriel stood. "Let us gather up some leaves. We will make a bed for you out here in the clearing. You will be able to lie down and enjoy the night sky."

"That would be wonderful," said Tobe.

Tobe put the finishing touches on his bed of leaves. "Fit for a king," he said, lying down.

Time passed as Tobe silently watched the night sky. Without him realizing it, he went deeper and deeper into the stillness of the night. So deep he went, that at one priceless instant, he felt a "pop." It was as if a transparent veil—pulled tight—had worn thin enough for him to break through! It was as if his ears had popped and he could hear clearly again, except that it was more than his ears—it was his eyes, heart, and being too!

Now the space of the night sky had such clarity and was saturated with *life—a life* of *Oneness*! His awareness merged and spread throughout this *life*. Now he could sense more clearly the depth between the stars. Yes, he found himself large—so large that the stars were no longer outside of him. It was as if he held the miracle and wonder of their existence within himself! Then he realized: *he was swimming in the River Is!*

Deep into the night, with his heart full to the brim, his eyelids, heavy from all the miracles he had seen that day, began to close. And he slipped into a deep and refreshing sleep—held safely in the arms of Inlăkesh.

CHAPTER ELEVEN

A Shadow in the River

*All we basically have to do is to be there, but simply, ardently,
the way the earth simply is, consenting to the seasons, light
and dark and all together in space, not asking to rest upon
anything other than the net of influences and forces in which
the stars feel secure.*

Rainer Maria Rilke

*Row, row, row your boat,
Gently down the stream.
Merrily, merrily, merrily, merrily,
Life is but a dream*

Author Unknown

 OBE'S EYES OPENED. STARS were still sparkling against the blush of the faint, warm light of dawn. Auriel, softly lit and sitting on the rock, faced the coming sunrise.

"Don't you ever sleep, Auriel?"

Auriel stretched and sighed. "Mm-m-m . . . every now and then." She glanced at Tobe. "Are you ready for another day in Inlăkesh?"

Tobe could not imagine a day more incredible than the day before. "Oh, yes!"

As they watched the approaching dawn, Tobe realized that Auriel and he shared a most precious gift: they did not always have to speak; they were not afraid of silence. Their eyes, their expressions, even their stillness could say nearly everything that needed to be said, and often better than words.

Lights were glowing in many of the homes of the village. People were beginning their day.

"They are *waking up* . . . in the River," said Auriel. "Can you feel it, Tobe?"

"Yes."

Tobe sat silently, watching the silhouettes of birds fly across the soft, luminous sky, their calls joined by the occasional distant barking of a dog and the crowing of a rooster—the sounds clear in the thin air of early dawn. Forms in the landscape began to emerge from the shadows of night, displaying faint washes of color. Homes and farms became visible, hills and trees distinct.

Moments passed, and the pale light on the horizon grew brighter, giving the sky its first touch of blue, into which the stars started fading away. The bottoms of little gray clouds slowly took on a rose-colored blush and then turned orange and then back to pure golden, the exact same progression Tobe remembered from the sunset, but in reverse.

Then a brilliance too bright to look upon peeked over the mountains. Wondrous sun had come to claim its day! The force of its radiance, after the deep, dark quiet of the night, was piercing, yet also soothing.

Here is a different order of creation altogether. Look how it expresses itself in pure radiance! And how like a god it freely extends its life to everything it lights upon! That it can even touch on this world of solid things at all is nothing short of a miracle!

The sun continued to rise; the clouds turned to pure glowing white, and the sky grew rich and awake with the color blue.

"What a wonderful time of day," Tobe exclaimed.

"Yes, it *is* magnificent," replied Auriel. "And through it all, the River Is continues to flow, *constant—never changing*. We are very blessed, Tobe, to be able to experience *both* worlds together."

Tobe felt a wave of gratitude to Auriel for the way she kept bringing him back to the River—and he loved her for it.

They got up and began preparing a bit of breakfast. Tobe built a fire, and from his backpack he got his old metal cup. "As good as the finest painted porcelain," he said. He made some tea that they shared. Auriel took out some crumpets and jam that the baker in Góndāwă had given her. They sat there eating their breakfast and enjoying the morning. Then they put out the fire, gathered up their things, and went light-footedly down the hill.

As they walked, Tobe said, "I had the most curious dreams last night—you know, the kind with a lot of detail—the kind where you can even see the color and texture of the individual threads in things—that kind of dream. Maybe our dreams are often like that, but we are not aware of it.

"Anyway, last night I dreamt of a horse and then went galloping away on it. Its muscles were flexing and its hoofs were pounding on the earth. Every hair in the horse's mane was flying wildly in the wind—all in amazing detail! It all seemed as real as this," Tobe said, gesturing at the landscape before them.

"I know," said Auriel. "The mind can create on a huge scale too. It can dream an immense canyon, or even the vast cosmos of stars in the night sky. It can dream a whole town and fill it with people, all busy and moving about. And your mind can make a dream of a 'you' in an endless variety of scenes, interacting with others."

Again, Tobe was impressed with Auriel's intelligence.

This is no child.

He looked closer at her, trying to decipher some clue as to her true nature, something beyond her adolescent form, but he could not see past it. Her reality remained a mystery, for all he saw were her childish eyes, sparkling and smiling back at him.

Tobe continued, "Last night, I also had another dream of a torrential downpour, with hundreds of thousands of individual raindrops falling in a fierce wind. I dreamt of growing rivulets eroding the soil, along with a myriads of rocks—down to the smallest pebble, as parts of a whole mountain were washed away. The sounds of it all made everything so believable. After the storm, I dreamt of the sun coming out, glowing in all its brilliance, warming my flesh. In my dream, I created a sun in my own mind!

"And the strangest dream of all was that I cut my hand and it bled. I could even look into the cut. In my dream, I saw the muscles and bone there! Nowhere was there a gap or chink where the dream was not—where the light of our normal waking world could shine through and show me that I was only dreaming. Everything held together and made 'complete sense'—even though it was made of nothing—a mere dream in a mind! Not once did I ever suspect the illusion of it all and that I was dreaming."

"It's curious," added Auriel, "the way everything in our dreams behaves the way it does in this world. When things fall, they shatter and pieces go flying, exactly as they should. The mind portrays flowing water, rising fog, and the flights of birds—all doing what they should do, without the slightest flaw. And all this the mind does with the greatest of ease."

Auriel leaned over and lightly touched Tobe and said, "You must keep looking at the power of the mind to create a world in your dreams. It is so important in understanding what this world is. Mighty lessons are moving your way now. I feel it. Come, we have places to go."

They traveled along. The earth turned soft, made mostly of clay and sand. This was a land of strong-willed plants, more infrequent in number—tufts of golden grasses and the occasional smaller wildflower. Light bluish-green shrubs of sage added their scent to the air. Cacti became more common, their pointy needles protecting their precious moisture, yet freely offering their blossoms—gifts of sweet nectar for birds and bees, and color for the eye.

Over eons, the infrequent but forceful downpours had created whimsical shapes in the landscape—arched gables, flying buttresses, spires, and statues—some as if ready to topple over. Others, like enormous pointy fingers, balanced huge rocks on their tips with ease.

The ground appeared to "flow" and build into large waves, frozen in time, cresting and about to break. Small, round evergreen trees "rode" these waves of earth. Upon these waves, Auriel and Tobe joyfully traveled from crest to bottom and to crest again.

A brown hawk made graceful arcs as it soared above, rising up into a billowy kingdom of clouds, with folds large enough to hold canyons. Tobe marveled at the hawk and felt a touch of envy. *Ah, to be able to fly like that, through such vast volumes of space—and on wings made of feathers, no less!* Then he remembered the mighty River Is, and he realized how truly fortunate he was. *I do not need feathers to fly!*

Tobe thought of the River and longed to go for a swim. He called It. It immediately responded and he dove in. As he swam, he not only became aware that love, light, and awareness were in the River, but this time there was also something new. Some kind of intelligence was in It. He could feel his mind merge and expand into this "intelligence." It immediately sharpened his intuitions and inspired his creative thought.

This time it was a short swim for Tobe. After it ended, he started thinking about what he had seen. "Is there something like a 'mind' in the River?" he asked Auriel.

"The River is Mind . . . as It is many other things."

Tobe was silent as he contemplated Auriel's words.

"Tobe, you have only just begun to fathom the wonders of this land. There is another thing I need to tell you. It is one of the greatest mysteries of Inlãkesh. And after your dreams last night, I think you are ready."

"There is something else?!" Tobe said with a lighthearted smile.

"Remember the details in your dreams?" continued Auriel. "Now look around and ask yourself if this is any different. Ask 'What if Inlãkesh exists like a dream in a mind?'"

Tobe pondered it. "Oh, Auriel, it's impossible. We have traveled long through Inlãkesh. I have touched it and breathed it. To me it is very real and solid."

"What if it were but a dream of 'solid.' What if space and time, too, were a dream?" replied Auriel. "Mind is much more powerful than you can imagine."

Suddenly Tobe's expression changed, "It *is* odd, but . . . I have had a strange sensation here in Inlãkesh. At times it feels like I am awake in a dream. But in no way did I ever imagine . . ."

Then a smile came to Tobe, "Yet, what if it were all in a mind—an amazing Mind! That would be utterly and completely . . . *astonishing*! But . . . no . . . surely that can't be."

Tobe began to feel nervous. It seemed as if his whole world, as he knew it, could at any moment unravel, replaced by something he was not sure was even possible.

"Call Inlãkesh 'real,'" said Auriel, "and it will be real to you. Call it a 'dream' and you will see it AS IT IS. It is only your belief that makes it appear 'real.' That is the power of your belief."

Then Tobe had another thought. "But it can't be my mind that is creating all this," he said. "Inlãkesh existed . . . you existed even before I came here."

"Of course. There is also a collective mind thing going on," Auriel responded, "where people are dreaming together. This gives rise to the whole shared dreamscape of Inlãkesh . . . and the world, even. I have been dreaming myself through time, just as you have. Our dreams are touching now, in time. But, like I said, what if time, too, was a dream?

"There is more to this dream idea, but it can wait. Don't try to figure it out with your little mind. That will never do. It is the wrong tool and would be no fun at all!"

Tobe could hardly wait to hear more. So many pieces seemed missing to this dazzling and unbelievable puzzle of Inlăkesh.

Auriel rose and looked at Tobe. "Insights will come as you swim in the River. Let *experience* teach you. Keep things simple. Don't force anything. Just gently tell yourself as often as you can as we move through Inlăkesh: 'I see a world. It exists only in Mind—like a dream at night,' and see what happens. Most importantly, have fun."

Auriel started walking and Tobe followed. "But, Auriel, what about the River? I *did* swim in the River . . . surely that was no dream."

"You are right," said Auriel. "It was no dream. The River flows in the dream, and it flows beyond, in the Mind. It is everywhere. It is the very life of the Mind, and the very life out of which our dreams are woven. But these are just words, Tobe. You need to *EXPERIENCE* it.

"Be ready to be lifted up at any moment into new vistas of Mind that will astonish you! You never know what will trigger a glimpse into the nature of Mind. One way to start is by stepping back into the River. Go ahead. Swim in the River. Be open and see what happens."

Tobe saw the River flowing everywhere, and he slid into It. His awareness sharpened. The body could no longer hold him. His being expanded into the River . . . and then into what felt like some kind of Mind. *Like a vast Ocean of Mind!*

Deep in the River, he looked out at Inlăkesh and on all the life forms of the landscape—birds, deer, coyotes, ground squirrels, insects, clouds, and trees. In an instant, Tobe had the most unexpected and bizarre experience. The images of Inlăkesh did not rest upon an exterior world at all! Incredibly, they were images in this Mind—like holograms projected into a dreamscape—all hovering in this vast Mind!

How is this possible?!

"This Mind is holy and limitless!" Tobe could hear Auriel say, "It contains all minds and their individual dreams."

As Tobe moved deeper into the revelation of Mind, this Mind felt increasingly holy. He saw the deepening perfection of things around him. Everything resonated with purity, light, and love—interacting in total harmony within this field of Mind.

It seemed to Tobe that he was looking at some well-made watch—a cosmic, watch, alive and on a huge scale, with all the gears and pieces precisely spinning and turning—ticking in time, creating the intricate, orderly design of the dream of Inlăkesh. And Tobe felt the Love of the River flowing through it all.

The Dream of a World in a Holy Mind

Tobe's awareness entered back into his body. He stood speechless next to Auriel. Finally he said, "The Mind is glorious beyond imagining . . . and this world is more wondrous than I could have ever envisioned."

A bird came to rest on a nearby branch as Auriel and Tobe passed. Its happy, crystal-clear warble filled the air. Tobe stopped and looked. This bird was such a delightful wonder to look upon with its sparkling eyes, delicate feathers, and its tiny, jointed talons holding firm to the branch. Its life and its exquisite appearance, too, were pure perfection. He felt the sublime mystery of the bird's existence, taking his breath away, as he began to sense the intelligence and will of Mind projecting the bird's form into the mental landscape of Inlăkesh.

Tobe turned towards Auriel. "Everything is much more than it seems, and the miracle of what's going on we don't even suspect."

Auriel, smiling, looked at Tobe and said, "Your life now will be even more astounding as you watch the Mind, which is also yours, dreaming this world."

Tobe stood there looking in amazement at Inlăkesh. "Is there any more incredible vision to see than the dreaming of the world?"

A soft glow came to Auriel's smile, "Oh, yes indeed, there is: the vision of what you really *ARE*!"

The next happy days passed effortlessly, one into another, as Auriel and Tobe walked through Inlăkesh, enjoying the life of the River together. Though Tobe could not hold the realization for long, how curious it was for him to walk on ground that was no more than a dream, with dream legs, no less, while all of Inlăkesh hovered in his vast mind. This was way beyond his ability to comprehend, but he did not worry about that. *Living it—that is the thing!*

It became easier for Tobe to call the River now. Just a gentle affirmation was all that was needed. He found he never left the River for long. Most of the time, he was in It, though It was often somewhere in the background. Yet, It always held him securely.

The day had been rich. Time had passed quickly. They had been hiking all morning, and it was time for a break.

"There is a good spot," said Auriel pointing to a tree on a stone ledge.

They made their way to the ledge, which overlooked a plain and a stream far below. A soft whistling sound startled Tobe as it shot by his head. Tobe looked. It was the sound of air moving across the feathers of a black raven as it swooped past, close enough for Tobe to touch. It seemed like a spirit—it felt like an omen. Tobe sensed something important was coming.

As they sat in the shade of a juniper tree, Tobe said, "Today is special. Nothing I can put my finger on, yet."

Auriel was quiet for a moment and then said, "Tobe, you must prepare yourself . . ."

Everything in Tobe stopped. There was something in Auriel's tone he had never heard before. His attention was on her every word.

"You must prepare yourself," she repeated and then added, ". . . to return to Soñadora."

Her words were like an anxious hand, grabbing and crumpling up Tobe's heart, filling him with dread. His day had quickly become anything but "special."

With anxiety welling up inside, Tobe said, "But I can't . . . I can't. I'm not . . . ready."

"I'm sorry," said Auriel.

Tobe looked away, "I don't want to go back. I can't live without the River!"

"It will go with you . . . *wherever* you go."

All was still for a moment, and then Auriel continued, "You have experienced how the River loves you. Well, It loves everyone with the same intensity. It wants everyone to find the happiness It has freely given you. Those on the edge of the world are especially in need of happiness—real, lasting happiness."

"But here it is easy and natural to swim with others," said Tobe. "Here, everyone knows of their true nature in the River. Why would I ever want to swim and merge with anyone back in Soñadora, where fear and hate live and multiply so easily in their hearts?"

"The River will make everyone whole and one with each other in Soñadora, just as it does here," replied Auriel. "Everyone there will shine as brightly as anyone here in Inlãkesh. Go and see for yourself—go and see the transformation of your world!"

"Is such a change *truly* possible in a world like Soñadora . . .," Tobe asked, "where minds are so closed? The people in Soñadora are fearful of the unknown. They consider it utter nonsense even to think of anything that lies beyond the little world their senses show them. I know. I used to be like them. If I told them about the joys of discovering who they are in the River, and how large and glorious they are, they would only laugh."

"You understand so much now," replied Auriel. "You know both worlds: Soñadora and Inlãkesh—and you know what it is like to swim in the River. You have much to offer them, and they need you. Many *are* becoming dissatisfied with their world and are ready now to listen. They are beginning to suspect that there must be something greater. More and more of them will listen as time passes, and they see the changes in those around them who *have* awakened in the River."

Tobe was not convinced.

Auriel's words began to flow with more emphasis. "And they *will* listen, because you will be speaking a language they know deeply within their hearts and have not totally forgotten. As with you, before they were born in Soñadora, they too freely rode the River. It was their *home*, too, and just as with you, they too forgot and fell deeply asleep in the dream of the world.

"Riding the River is in their very nature. You see, they used to ride the River with you. What a sight that was, and it will happen again some day!

"That, Tobe, is why, in time, they *will* listen. Don't worry. You will know what to say and what to do, for the River will show you."

Tobe started to feel his resistance falling away. He was beginning to hear what Auriel was trying to say. She was right. It was not just about himself anymore. Things needed doing; help was needed. No doubt it would be disappointing at times, but he *could* do it. He would see to it the best he could.

"I will go back to Soñadora," he said.

Auriel gave him a big hug. "Thank you," she said. "Wherever you go, let your heart lead you. It knows the way. It knows the River."

As Tobe looked about, everything seemed even more special, now that he knew he had to leave Inlăkesh. Suddenly the impulse to ride the River filled him.

"Going for a swim will clear up my mind, as it always does," he told Auriel.

Auriel suddenly seemed a little anxious. She looked deep into Tobe's eyes and said, "Before you do, I want to let you know how much you are loved here in Inlăkesh."

Tobe was a bit perplexed; something seemed to be disturbing Auriel. She was not quite herself. Then he told himself it was just a passing thing and gave it no more thought. He called the River and dove in.

"Have a good swim, dearest Tobe," Auriel called out.

The life of the River instantly flowed into him, refreshing every part of his being. He swam joyously in the River, on and on. There were so many levels to the River. Tobe blissfully swam through them all. To him, all the levels were equally glorious, for he saw Love and Light shining through each and every one of them!

Then something peculiar caught his attention, something he had never seen before in the River. First It appeared as a shadow. Then It became larger and larger as It came closer. *As big as a house! No, way bigger even!!* Now he could see It—a huge eye, a body that appeared to be covered in scales and with giant fins: *The Great Fish!*

An orange glow emanated all about It. Its body was transparent here and there, as if It did not belong to this world. Along Its sides crackled little sparks and streaks of blue lightning. It swam right toward Tobe. He did not need a fishing pole or bait—*he* would do just fine! Then, in one quick darting lunge, the jaws of The Great Fish opened wide and swallowed Tobe whole, with no problem at all.

Tobe rolled and fell deep into The Great Fish. Everything was in a state of confusion for a second or two. As he tumbled, he felt he was dissolving. *What's happening?! What am I becoming?*

Things started to settle and come to rest. Tobe took stock of himself. He was no worse for wear. He stood up inside The Great Fish, with room to spare. Inside The Great Fish, it was dark, but slowly things started to stand out. The Great Fish was much larger than one would think possible. Inside was vast space—really, really vast space. Tobe started to see that it contained the whole of Inlākesh. In fact, it contained the dream of the whole world, as well as other worlds, stars, and galaxies of stars!

There were also other dimensions and plains of reality inside *The Great Fish—and even Heaven too!* It held *All There Is!* And through It all, the River flowed. Then came the miracle, impossible to describe. As Tobe looked in wonder upon The Great Fish, in that instant, he became one with It and all It held. He realized that he was *looking on his Self!*

"*TOBE, YOU ARE EVERYTHING,*" said a voice echoing throughout The Great Fish.

Tobe was held in timelessness before the vision, and then the experience started to fade.

"Welcome," said a thought in Tobe's mind. But Tobe knew it wasn't his thought.

Tobe would come to discover that not only could The Great Fish communicate like that, but in a rich variety of fascinating ways. Sometimes The Great Fish would express Itself through images in Tobe's mind while he was either awake or sleeping; or with waves of emotion that moved through Tobe's heart and body. Sometimes The Great Fish could speak with a loud voice, reverberating in Tobe's chest, or with a soft whisper in his ear. The Great Fish would also use symbols, sometimes large, with an intricate geometric pattern, all glowing and hovering. Tobe was surprised that he could understand these symbols with no problem at all. It could also communicate in light, which Tobe could read like a book.

Tobe found that his body was right in front of one of the eyes of The Fish, looking out upon the world. It was like a big, round window. He was surprised how much sharper and clearer everything appeared through this window—how enchanting, and delightful.

The Great Fish started to move. Its tail flicked and Its body rose—up and up.

Tobe saw the River clearly expanding and rising—wider and higher before them. The Great Fish began to swim in the River's living current. Down below, he saw beloved Auriel. She was waving.

So she knew!

It appeared the corners of her mouth were quivering slightly, betraying her smile—but he was not sure because of the distance. He thought, too, he may have seen a twinkle of a tear in her eye, but it was hard to tell, for at the same time, her eyes were so full of light and joy.

The Great Fish swam quickly, high over the landscape, and before long they were over the village of Góndăwă. Farther on, they passed over the fisherman far below, standing on the sandbank with fishing pole in hand. He was looking up in a state of complete wonder.

The Great Fish continued on. They passed through a large circle of rope. Tobe looked down and saw the cowgirl twirling her lasso. Then, a second or two later, just outside The Fish, close enough to touch, he saw Aban, the Borderland Man, tumbling and turning joyfully in the current of the River as The Great Fish sped on.

They soared in a westerly direction, The Great Fish riding the crest of a wave of the River Is as It continued to expand before them. Tobe saw the beaches of Inlăkesh as they gave way to what seemed like an ocean.

How unreal it looks.

Then Inlăkesh disappeared altogether, as The Great Fish entered the clouds.

Tobe Looking Out of the Eye of The Great Fish

CHAPTER TWELVE

Return to Soñadora

*How do drops of water know themselves to be a river? Yet the
river flows on.*

Antoine de Saint-Exupéry

*Why who makes much of a miracle?
As to me I know of nothing else but miracles,
To me every hour of the light and dark is a miracle,
Every cubic inch of space is a miracle.*

Walt Whitman, *Miracles*

 OBE LOOKED OUT OF the eye of The Great Fish. The clouds
had finally parted. He could see another world below.
It was a starker kind of desert land, with barren peaks
and ridges surrounding a flat plain. *It seems familiar.*

He was then surprised to see the stone precipice
where the Bookseller and he spoke, and where he discovered the portal to Inlăkesh. He saw specks off in the
distance. His heart sank. *The carnival.* He felt a turn-
ing in his stomach. His heart ached for Inlăkesh. *I have returned to my old
world!*

The River suddenly came to a standstill, as if barred by an invisible dam. The Great Fish then came to a stop at the very edge of the River and hovered.

Why did the River stop?

The Great Fish replied, "Your eyes cannot see the River flowing because your heart is too closed to your old world."

Tobe did not understand how such a simple thing as a closed heart could stop the great River. Yet one thing he had learned by now was that if something sounded too simple to be true, it was most likely very true. And if it sounded impossible, it was most definitely possible.

Tobe grew confused. "What do you mean, my heart is closed?" Tobe asked aloud.

The voice responded, "In your heart, how do you see the people of the carnival?"

Tobe thought for a moment and then answered as truthfully as he could, "Well, they are a proud people—vain and often stubborn. Though they have their good traits, they are mostly self-centered. They are full of self-destructive urges. Though at times they can be kind, they are prone to unbridled bouts of hate and anger, attacking others as well as themselves. They are . . ."

"Enough. *That* is the voice of a closed heart."

Tobe was silent.

"Step back into the River, and let the *River* show you *how* to look on the people of the carnival."

Tobe was relieved that he didn't have to change his heart alone—that the River would do it. Tobe became still. He turned his attention to the River and felt Its presence growing. He merged into the River and began to swim. Almost immediately, Tobe started to sense the Love in the River, and the Love flowed into him, filling his heart. His eyes began to look out at a very different world.

As he looked, Tobe started to see that the people of the carnival were not at all the way they first appeared. What he had judged in them was no more than an outer shell of them. It was not the real thing at all. Beneath their self-pride, vanity, stubbornness, their hate and anger, he started to see something magnificent, pure, and glorious dawning in his awareness. Yes, they were much, much more—something vast and incredibly magnificent! They, too, were part of the life of the River, pure and perfect in every way.

The more Tobe saw, the more his heart opened. As his heart opened, the River began to flow, growing stronger. Soon it was a mighty torrent, heading towards the carnival.

"You are right! Look at It flow!" exclaimed Tobe.

The waves of the River surged through the carnival, washing down every aisle and into every tent, flowing around everyone and everything. As the River swelled, It made everything whole and magnificent in Tobe's eyes.

"The *'impossible'* is happening," Tobe marveled. "This old world is *changing*!

"I must go down there."

The mouth of The Great Fish opened, and Tobe dashed out. He made his way down from the ledge through scree and boulders. In no time, he was across the flat plain and making his way through the opening in the fence where the Bookseller had taken him. He was approaching the Bookseller's tent when he stepped out.

"I thought I felt the River growing stronger," said the Bookseller, beaming. "Welcome back! I see you've been swimming in the River . . .," he glanced up into the sky, "and riding The Great Fish!"

"It is good to see *you*," said Tobe. "I never thought I would say this, and even a few minutes ago I would have been unable to say it, but it's good to be back at the carnival—and especially, to see the River flowing through it."

"Yes, isn't it startling how different it looks in the River?" said the Bookseller.

They both stood there silently, looking at the carnival. "Heading back to Soñadora?" asked the Bookseller.

"Yes."

The Bookseller smiled. "Come, let's go see how the River touches on this world."

They walked down the isle of tents. The carnival was jammed with people, just as before. Everyone seemed to be enjoying the day. The carnival was a happy place again, a place to have fun and play for a while. It was more like how Tobe remembered when he first arrived at the carnival, before the nightmares came. Yet it was also different now. Tobe noticed that when people passed and their eyes met, in many there was a depth of kindness in their eyes—a beauty. They smiled with a warmth that he had never seen on any face before in the carnival. Everything, too, seemed less heavy—bathed in a light. Tobe could not help but feel happy.

As they walked, Tobe thought of his friend. "Have you ever heard of a fellow named 'Sebastian'?"

"Yes," said the Bookseller. "He comes in quite often to buy books, mostly by poets or mystics. He went off to some war—became a hero. He helped free an oppressed people from some bloody tyrants. He saved many lives."

Tobe was relieved. Shaking his head he said, "This is the strangest world."

"Yes, that's for sure," replied the Bookseller. "Sebastian teaches philosophy now at the University at the other end of the carnival. His students speak highly of him. Lately, when he comes into my tent, our conversations go to some very deep places. He is beginning to realize that there is much more to life. That the River is flowing here will not be a surprise to him."

"Tell him hello for me," said Tobe. "If I had more time, I would love to see him, but The Great Fish and Soñadora are waiting."

"I will tell him. Our walk should not take long."

Tobe's thoughts turned to an earlier time. "I remember that night when we sat out overlooking the carnival, and you said that a light shines in the carnival—a light that shines through everything with such power."

Looking around, Tobe added, "I see what you mean now."

They passed the Money Tent where people were still playing their games, and then the Political Booths where things were much quieter.

As Tobe looked closer at the people, he started to feel confused. "The radiant life of the River surrounds everyone, yet on some faces I still see suffering—I see an anxiousness. Some are still covering up the same deep-seated emptiness and fear I saw here before. I was hoping that the River would really transform this world and touch them all. I imagined they would be so different somehow—like the people in Inlākesh."

"Oh, the River *is* changing them," exclaimed the Bookseller, "changing their lives as we speak. For many, it may not be obvious yet, but one thing you can count on is that the River will eventually have its way. You will see. This is just the very beginning, Tobe."

The Bookseller and Tobe walked past Role Town, where people were still playing their roles. Tobe noticed a charm about the place now. To Tobe, people seemed more at peace in what they were doing. It did remind him a little bit of Góndāwă. But he wasn't sure if the people had really changed or if he was just looking with the eyes of the River.

As they strolled down the next isle, the Bookseller asked, as he pointed ahead, "Do you remember this tent?"

"Oh yes," replied Tobe. "Oh yes, indeed—the Love Tent."

They approached the tent. As the Bookseller and Tobe walked through the heart-shaped entrance and joined the crowd, the Bookseller said, "The River is touching them. They *will* realize it. What they feel for each other will grow. Their relationships will become so loving that it will even astonish *them*!"

As Tobe looked around, he was surprised at the depth of love he was already starting to see. Again, he wasn't sure if it was just him or if that was the way it was.

"Their relationships," continued the Bookseller, "will become a portal for a love, itself, to come into this world, flowing everywhere."

Tobe could not quite imagine it, even though he knew the power and love of the River well. Yet, he had long ago given up on being the arbiter of what was possible and what was not. Things were too glorious and unfathomable for that!

Tobe smiled. "Let's see what else the River is doing."

When the Bookseller and Tobe got to where the dancing girls had been, the drunken crowd was nowhere to be seen. The stage stood silent. Tobe was disappointed. He was hoping to see the girl again—the petite one with amber hair. He wanted to see if she was different—and how he might see her now. Just as they turned to leave, she passed by.

She took a second look at Tobe and said, "I wondered what had happened to you. You were different from the others."

Tobe was surprised that she remembered him. He said nothing, looking upon her without need or want. She *did* seem different. Her eyes looked clearer. There was now a faint glow about her.

As they spoke, without knowing how, Tobe left his body. The dancing girl and he began to swim and spin in the River together, as pure energy.

Then Tobe remembered that The Great Fish was waiting. With that thought, their swim suddenly came to an end, and Tobe entered back into his bodily form.

"That was grand . . . swimming together," said Tobe.

"Swimming? Together?" was her only reply. She stood, looking perplexed.

The Bookseller lightly touched Tobe on the arm. "It's time to go," he said as he started walking away.

Tobe and the girl looked each other in the eyes one last time as she said, "It was nice to see you again."

Tobe took her hand gently in his. "You know, you are much more than 'pretty.'" He remembered his swim with her. "You are *beautiful*!" At that, he let her hand gently slip from his. He then turned and caught up to the Bookseller.

As they walked away, Tobe glanced back. The dancing girl appeared bewildered.

"How is that possible," Tobe asked the Bookseller, "that I could swim with her in the River . . . and she not even know it? Why are things so complicated here—so different from Inlăkesh, where you swim with others and *they know it.*"

"One day she, too, will be awake and swim in the River. It is her true nature, after all."

They passed The War Tent. There was still a line to go in, but it was smaller now.

"It won't be long before this tent will finally be taken down," the Bookseller said.

Even after all the amazing things Tobe had seen and gone through, he still found *that* hard to believe. "Is it really possible?" Tobe wondered aloud. "What a different carnival it would be then, without hate and war upon it!"

"When we are all one in the River," said the Bookseller, "who is there to fight, after all? We are on the verge of the changing of a world!"

They passed by the exit of the carnival with its somber black-draped fabric, its wreaths, and its caskets all in a row. A sad melody still filled the air, paying homage to death. The light of the River had not touched these breaking hearts yet. Tobe looked at all the grief-stricken faces. How curious it seemed to him now—what a tragic misunderstanding about the nature of things.

He knew now, without a doubt, that in the River there is no death. Yes, he knew that the pain of loss would still be there, but how different it would be, just as it was for the people in Inlăkesh.

The last tent they came to was The Hall of Mirrors. Tobe stopped. "I need to see one more thing."

Tobe entered the tent and went up the ramp. The mirrors portrayed him all wavy and distorted just as before—in each mirror, again, a different mood and condition. However, now his image appeared almost transparent, with light behind, shining through. When Tobe came to the last mirror—"The Time Mirror," all he saw was an intense light—vast and full of peace. Love, too, was in the light. Tobe studied it for quite a while.

Wonderful!

Relieved, he turned and went out to where the Bookseller was waiting.

Carnival III—The River Transforming the Carnival

On the way back to the Bookseller's tent, Tobe felt a deep wave of emotion and said to the Bookseller, "Thank you, for *all* you have done."

"I know great things are awaiting you in Soñadora." The Bookseller glanced in the direction of his tent. "Wait here. I have a gift for you."

The Bookseller quickly disappeared into his tent. In no time, he was back carrying something. He handed it to Tobe.

"I think you will be able to appreciate it now," said the Bookseller.

Tobe took it. It was the Bookseller's curious painting. Now Tobe could easily make it out. It was not a vase, after all. It was The Great Fish, clear as day, with the orange glow all about It and blue lightning shooting across Its side. It had an eye, sharp and focused, that could "see everything."

"It's a remarkable painting," said Tobe. "Thank you. I will cherish it always."

"Well, I best be going," said Tobe glancing up towards The Great Fish in the distance. "There are things to do!"

They embraced. Tobe turned and made his way to the edge of the carnival, where he slipped through the hole in the fence. He hiked across the flat plain and then up to where The Great Fish hovered. Its mouth opened wide. Tobe turned and looked back at the carnival.

Tobe felt his confidence growing. *If such a change can happen in this place, it can surely happen in Soñadora.*

He thought of the Bookseller and Sebastian, and then Auriel, the Borderland Man, the Cowgirl, the Fisherman, and even the people of the carnival. *Such extraordinary characters are in this world. I have been fortunate to know them all.*

Tobe stepped inside The Great Fish and made his way to the round window of the eye. The mouth of the Fish closed, and then, with a swish of Its tail, It rose into the air with the carnival fading in the distance.

As the River advanced and The Great Fish continued, Tobe looked down at the ground, searching for dark holes and the Bubble People. He could find neither, but he did see what appeared like a few discarded bubbles rolling about in the wind.

The vast expanse of desert began to give way to trees growing larger, hills rising taller, and the color of sand and clay turning into the lush greenness of meadows.

"Though it appears as if the River is spreading before us now," said the voice inside The Great Fish, "that is an illusion of sorts. In truth, It has *always* been *here* and *everywhere*. It is only your awareness of It, Tobe, that is spreading, allowing you to see It now. Your whole journey to Inlăkesh was about giving you the eyes to see It."

Soon the landscape started to appear familiar. Tobe could see the road he had traveled on, heading east. He could make out his neighbor's pasture and barn below and . . . his own home!

MY HOME!

MY OWN HOME!

He was overjoyed but profoundly befuddled.

It makes no sense; I saw it burn!

Even from high above, he could see that someone had taken care of things while he was gone. No tall weeds were visible; the shrubs had been clipped, and the garden had been tended.

Oh, sweet home, though I don't know what happened the night you burned, it is sure good to see you still standing!

His home grew smaller in the distance as the River kept flowing, and The Great Fish kept swimming closer to the village of Soñadora. Tobe could now make out his dory, tied up securely to the pier. His heart went out to it, for he loved his dory. He could not wait to take her out on the lake—to cast a net, and do a sketch or two.

The River now surged over the last hill and down into the village of Soñadora, flowing around and through every lane and building, transforming it all to glowing. Back on the crest of the hill, The Great Fish hovered just above the ground. It opened Its mouth, letting in the daylight of Soñadora.

Tobe lingered before the eye-window of The Great Fish. He was in no hurry to leave. In the peaceful silence, he studied the village below. Tobe had a strong urge to stay in The Great Fish. He felt so vast in The Fish; he understood so much there.

Thoughts about the challenges that lay before him started to enter his mind, turning his heart all fluttery.

I don't think I can do this. Tobe could not move. *Another dark hole.*

"Yes, that is right. 'Tobe' can't do this," said the voice, "but the River *can.* The River is your strength now!"

With those words, Tobe's doubts instantly vanished away; his heart lightened. He began to feel that it was time to go. He had a life to live in Soñadora.

Then the voice continued, "Time is very different in Inlăkesh. Three years have gone by since you left Soñadora. Things have changed here. There are people who are now ready for you to show them the wonders of the River.

"Many have worried about you since you've been gone, especially Kallee. There will be much happiness in the village tonight."

Tobe slipped the Bookseller's painting into his backpack and walked towards the mouth of The Fish. He stepped down onto the lush grass. He felt his extraordinary adventure had all too quickly come to an end. He wished it could last forever.

Then a happy thought came: *This is the beginning of another great adventure—perhaps even more miraculous!*

His feet delighted to stand upon the familiar earth of Sonadora once again. He looked at the fields and animals grazing below. The barns and farmhouses seemed more immaculate than he remembered, the village in the distance more pristine. Tobe took in a deep breath. The old familiar scents of Soñadora—the wild flowers, cedars, and pines—entered him, their aromas swirling and dancing inside him, turning his inner world to joy.

He was surprised at the depth of the love welling up inside him for Soñadora. The bond he felt flowed deeper in his veins than he had realized. It was as if everything good about Soñadora had been wrapped up carefully and stored for safekeeping in a hidden place in his heart, without his knowing.

With a smile, he sighed. *It is good to be home!*

Tobe turned toward The Great Fish and looked into Its huge eye. It was like looking into a deep, black pool that fell to *everywhere*. Tobe stretched out his hand to touch The Great Fish. Feelings rushed from Tobe's heart, down his arm, and out through his fingertips. Tobe was not surprised that when he touched The Great Fish, his hand passed through Its surface, for It was not of this world at all.

Then an image arose in Tobe's mind of a dream he had long ago. It was of a "toy" standing in a doorway—a toy that turned into a real boy sitting on a bed floating on a river.

"You see, Tobe," said the voice. "The dream was a gift too. You have always been loved. Nothing has been an accident."

"Thank you," Tobe said with all his heart.

Tobe turned around and watched the River filling and overflowing the village and the whole valley, and then spilling over into the Great Nothing!

The dark space of the Great Nothing began to fade completely away in the glowing light of the River Is—Its light saturating every inch of it.

Look, Soñadora no longer stands before the darkness of the Great Nothing, but before the radiance of Heaven!

Tobe heard the swishing sound of fins, and as he watched, The Great Fish lifted off. With one quick flip of Its tail, It darted away, riding the current of the River. Up, up It swam among the floating clouds and then headed west, disappearing into the light where the darkness of the Great Nothing once was.

Just at that moment, a yellow butterfly with a touch of iridescent blue on its wings flew by, glancing Tobe on the cheek as if to say "hello." He watched as it fluttered and started gliding down to the valley and the village of Soñadora below. He felt the urge to tag along. As they headed down together, suddenly the butterfly cut off to the side, and Tobe's gaze followed. That is when he saw her. Kallee was picking mushrooms on the hill at the edge of the forest.

He called out to her, and when she turned and saw him, they ran to each other. Tobe's heart was bursting as his arms joyfully wrapped around her. His breath paused. His heart then soared. His hands, in ecstasy "sang" as they touched her. Passion, like a torrent, flowed out of his lips in every kiss. It was almost more than he could bear!

They pulled apart just enough to look at each other. Kallee was beaming with happiness. She was more beautiful than he remembered. There was also a deeper inner beauty in her, which Tobe had never seen before.

Tobe was suddenly swimming deep in the River. He moved beyond his body. He watched Kallee's spirit spreading in magnificence through space while, at the same time, he saw their bodies standing on the ground! Their spirits moved toward each other and began spinning and blending together. As they swam deeper in the River together, they merged into *One*!

How glorious is this life we share!

The experience faded. They stood there, holding each other close. Tobe looked down to the village, thinking of all the people there. It was time to show them how to swim in the River.

"Kallee, we have some friends to see. You know how everyone loves a good story. Well, I have a very strange and most peculiar tale to tell, and I think everyone will find great enjoyment in its telling."

"Yes!" said Kallee. "Let's do it! I would love it!"

Kallee took Tobe's hand and playfully started running down the hill, pulling Tobe along.

"Come, Tobe, faster!" she cheerfully called out. "We have things to do . . . wonderful things!"

Tobe and Kallee Standing on the Edge of Heaven

"Inlăkesh," also written "In La Kesh," or "In Lakéch," is a phrase from the ancient Mayan culture. It has been translated to mean *you are my other*, *I am another yourself*, or *I am you*.

Visit Micah Sanger on his blog and website, www.4riveris.com, as well as his art website, www.perception4u.com.

Acknowledgments

I WOULD LIKE TO express my deep appreciation to some wonderful people who were instrumental in bringing a shine and sparkle to this book: Shanna Mac Lean, Mary Neighbour, Rosilee Winn, Richard Buzbee, Connie Salles, Lisa Rothrock, Rita Moazzami, Bobby Stone, and in loving memory of Judy Ficksman.

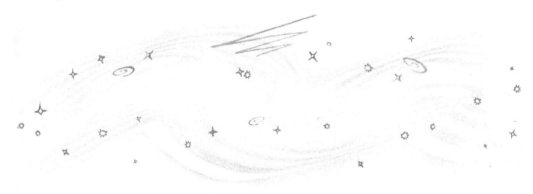

"Do you see the River? It is all around you."
Auriel

About the Author/Artist

I WAS BORN ON October 28th, 1950. My father was a country preacher and we lived in a dairy-farm community in Wisconsin. I was raised in a nurturing home with loving parents and two adorable older sisters. When I was six years old, my father joined the United States Army as a chaplain, and the family moved to France. During this time, we traveled throughout many parts of Europe. My parents enjoyed museums, and I was able to experience the highest expressions of religious and secular art, as well as the customs of many different cultures.

To go from the cow barns of Wisconsin to the gold and marble of the Vatican, to see Michelangelo's sculpture of Moses, were mind-opening experiences for a boy. I still have photographic memories of the veins on the marble arms of Moses.

Since then, I have lived in many parts of the United States. I first attended college at Clemson University, South Carolina, from 1969 to 1971. I took classes in literature and writing, and the focus of my studies made its progression from engineering to architecture and then finally to fine art studio, always following the trail that led to greater and greater freedom.

In 1971 I was drafted into the United States Army. I was fortunate to be given the position of illustrator on the General's Staff at Fort Sill, Oklahoma. Right before my discharge in 1973, I met and began my apprenticeship under the nationally known artist, Richard Goetz. I helped him in running his summer workshop in Santa Fe, New Mexico, that year.

In the early 1980s I continued my education at the University of California-Santa Barbara, and throughout the rest of the '80s at Chico State University, Chico, California. Through the years, I kept writing stories and poetry as I pursued my painting. I also kept studying and reading about the art of writing.

In 1997 I returned to the beautiful skies and landscapes of New Mexico. From 2002 to 2014, I was a security officer at the Los Alamos National Laboratory. It was a great job that allowed me time to observe in detail aspects of perception and states of awareness. Through the many hours of focused attention, often under conditions of isolation, some of my greatest insights and experiences have come. These insights have influenced my writing and painting to such a profound degree and have led to the development of my website, www.perception4u.com, followed by the the writing of this book.

Since the book was launched in 2016, it has received acclaim, winning the Ben Franklin Book Award, the Nautilus Book Award, the New Apple Book Award, and the Global eBook Award. The Nautilus Award was especially meaningful to me, winning it in the Memoir Category. This means that they realized, as fantastic as the tale is, that it is actually true; it is not just a made-up fairy tale but is based on *real* experiences. This is important to me because it will encourage the reader to feel and see the truth in what is written here, opening them up to their own rich experiences of the glorious River Is. And that is the point: to *experience* all this, for it is what we *ARE*.

I am now living in the quaint coastal town of Mendocino, California. It is an inspiring area in which to pursue my interest in writing and painting and to delve deeper into the mysteries of existence, of life, and its oneness—in this dimension and beyond. And if you happen to find yourself in this area, I would like to invite you to my studio for a visit during the times it is open.

Blessings to you, fellow travelers, and may your journey be overflowing with inexplicable joy and love.

Dear Reader,

Thank you for taking the time to read this book and give your attention to the artwork. I hope you enjoyed reading the book, as much as I enjoyed writing it. It was truly a wonderful experience.

Please tell your friends about it, and I would appreciate it if you took a moment to write a brief review of **Tobe and the River Is** *on Amazon.*

Thank you for your kindness.

Micah Sanger